THE PROCEDURE

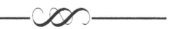

JEFFREY COHEN

Absolute Author
Publishing House

This book is a work of fiction.

Names, characters, places and

incidents are

the product of the author's imagination or

are used fictitiously.

Any resemblance to actual events,

locales or persons,

living or dead is coincidental.

Paperback: ISBN: 978-1-64953-374-6

EBook: ISBN: 978-1-64953-375-3

Audiobook: ISBN: 978-1-64953-376-0

Printed in the United States of America.

PROLOGUE

2022

The flashing ambulance lights could be seen as the rig hurtled down the DC streets. No need for a siren as the streets were mostly abandoned just past two a.m. That was fortunate, since the emergency vehicle skidded along its path on the icy, slick roads from the downpour which had started hours earlier.

It was pretty much a straight shot down Wisconsin Avenue from Georgetown to the Walter Reed National Military Medical Center. The storefronts were lighted, but most were closed. Combined with the bevy of streetlamps, visibility would have been easy were it not for the heavy raindrops that splashed against the windshield like giant tears from God. Every dip in the road created a waterfall sized spray that gave a homeless man his first shower in who knows how long.

There were four people in the belly of the speeding vehicle: two first responders, the patient and his frantic wife. It was packed with equipment, making it look like a miniaturized operating room. The walls were filled with monitors, IV bags, EKG leads, and drawers full of various medications. The portable ventilator was attached to the limp man laying helplessly on the stretcher which had carried him from his high-end Georgetown townhome.

"Can't you do something?" the wife screamed at the attendants as her husband gasped for more air.

The medical staff ignored her as they methodically administered their treatments and tests.

"You know who my husband is, right?" she continued.

One of the attendants reached for a portable phone and dialed the emergency room at Walter Reed.

"Late 40s, male, blood pressure 180 over 120, trouble breathing. We have him on the respirator but no other signs of trauma. Incoming in three minutes."

They reached the emergency room entrance in less than 15 minutes, but it seemed like hours to the man's hysterical wife. A nurse and the attending physician met the ambulance as the rear doors swung open. The stretcher glided out, followed by the other inhabitants. As they rapidly pushed the stretcher into the brightly lit medical center, the woman nearly tackled the attending trying to get his attention.

"You need to know who you're helping. This is Secretary Milton Simon. My husband should not be sick – he had The Procedure!"

CHAPTER 1

1993

They were the least likely to be best friends.

Chris came from a lower middle-class family. Six feet two inches, extremely fit, long blond hair tumbling over his shoulders, you would expect to see him on a surfboard, not in the library where he spent most of his time. He didn't party a lot but had an endearing look and personality. His father owned a small grocery store in their small town. His mom stayed home to take care of the domestic duties. He was eternally grateful for his scholarship, which afforded him the chance to attend Stanford University.

Milton could not be more different. He was four inches shorter and was already showing the signs of male pattern baldness. His father, a Stanford alumnus, eased his son's admission, despite his uninspiring grades. But Milton was a social butterfly. He had the gift of gab, which ingratiated him with many who fell into his sphere.

They met during their freshman year, by accident. A real accident. Milton, driving too fast in his brand-new Corvette, almost ran Chris over as he was cycling to the library.

"Glad your car has good brakes."

"You should be glad I have good reflexes," Milton replied.

"Where are you headed in such a hurry?"

"Off to meet friends at the O."

"The O?"

"It's what all of those in the know call it – it's the Oasis Beer Garden. It's not far-off campus on El Camino Real. Hop in, I'll buy you a beer. It's the least I could do for almost running you down."

"I have to go to the library, and I'm not 21."

"First of all, how many girls can you meet at the library and second, I have a pocket full of fake IDs. Just chain your bike against that tree, and we'll have just one beer and I'll bring you back. The library will still be there."

"I don't know, I have to keep my grades up to keep my scholarship."

"One beer isn't going to ruin your scholarship. Get in before I really run you over."

"Okay, one beer."

Chris hopped over the unopened door and slid into the passenger seat. Milton squealed rubber even before he got his seat belt fastened. Five minutes later they arrived at the O. Chris wobbled out of the car, still shaking from the roller coaster ride to the students' favorite watering hole.

Come on… what's your name?"

"Chris."

"Okay, come on, I'll introduce you to my friends, just don't tell them you were on the way to the library."

The O looked like it came from another place and time. It had been open for about 50 years, and not much had changed except the normal wear and tear. The entrance sign bore a picture of a palm tree with a "Welcome to the Oasis, world famous burgers & pizza" greeting. Would have been more natural in Key West than a Stanford hangout.

It was Happy Hour when the boys arrived and the place was humming. Standing room only. As Milton pushed his way past patrons to get to the bar, many stopped him for fist pumps or high fives. Chris followed close behind to avoid getting lost in the crowd. They finally squeezed their way into a place at the bar and Milton ordered two drafts. A few of his friends joined them, and he made introductions all around. He introduced Chris as his new friend and a newbie to the O.

One friend, Tyler, started peppering Chris with questions.

"What are you studying?"

"Chemistry and biology".

"A real Brainard. Where are you from?"

"A small town in Ohio, I'm sure you've never heard of it."

"How did you end up at Stanford?"

"I was lucky enough to win a scholarship here."

Milton interjected, "What is this, an interrogation?"

"Just trying to find out about your new best friend."

"Hey, I just met him. Almost ran him over. That's how we met. Anyway, he's a smart dude, and we might need his help with our studies someday. So give him a break."

"It's okay Milton, I'd like to hear a little bit about you guys."

One beer turned into four while the boys shared their short life stories, the recent jokes they heard, and the latest intelligence on available women on campus.

A couple of the guys had girlfriends already, but Milton was content with playing the field for a while. Chris was apparently too caught up with his studies to spend time looking for female companionship.

Milton shared his favorite new joke with the group.

"There were two brothers, one seven and one five. The seven-year-old says to his younger brother, 'It's time we learned how to swear, so I'll say hell and you say ass'. The younger brother says okay as they walk down to the kitchen for breakfast. When they get there their mother asks the seven-year-old what he wants for breakfast. He replied, 'Hell, I think I'll have Cheerios'. The mother immediately slaps his face, grabs him by the collar and drags him into his bedroom. She tells him to stay there until she gets him. She goes back to the kitchen and asks her younger son what he wants. He says, 'You can bet your ass I'm not going to ask for Cheerios!'"

They all broke into laughter at the punchline. Everyone always enjoyed Milton's latest jokes, and this was no exception. "Got any more?" one of his friends asked.

"Sorry, that's it for today," Milton replied.

"Hey Milton, thanks for the beers, but I really need to get back to campus. Can you take me, or should I grab a cab?" Chris asked.

"I'll take you. Guys, we've gotta go. See you Friday night."

As the two exited, they bumped into a striking coed as she entered. Even Chris was taken aback.

"Wow, do you know her?"

Not yet, but you can be assured I will soon," mused Milton. "She must be a newbie like you."

CHAPTER 2

As usual Chris was studying in his dorm when the phone rang. He had to rummage through dirty clothes, research papers, and several textbooks to find it.

"Hey, Chris – it's Milton. My Dad gave me a couple of fifty-yard line tickets to Saturday's game. Want to join?"

"Let me check my schedule...looks like I might be available."

"Don't get too excited, there's only ten thousand other people who want that ticket."

"Just kidding, that'd be fantastic. I've never been to a college game before."

"I'll pick you up at eleven, the game starts at one. And don't forget to wear red."

"Don't worry, I know the procedure. I've got to get back to studying now, we have an important guest lecturer next week that requires some advanced prep. See you Saturday."

Saturday couldn't come soon enough for Chris. Although he downplayed it on the phone, he was really excited about attending his first game. Eleven came and went and no Milton. Finally, at about 11:20 Milton showed up. Screeching to a stop about two feet from Chris he yelled, "Hop in, we're running late."

"What's this we business, you have a frog in your pocket?"

"Very funny. I know, it's my fault, but when I went to pick up the tickets from my Dad, he made me meet this important political contact. Said it would be important for my future."

"So your future is in politics?"

"Who knows, I'm pre-law now majoring in political science. I think my Dad wants me to be president one day."

"President of Stanford or the United States?"

"Knowing my Dad, probably both."

"Maybe you should start by running for student body president."

"That's a good idea, I'll think about it when I'm a junior."

"Well right now, think about keeping your eyes on the road, Mr. Andretti."

"Aye aye captain."

They arrived at the stadium in plenty of time to meet and greet dozens of Milton's friends. Everyone was wearing red and energized by the rivalry of playing Notre Dame. When they finally reached their seats, right on the fifty-yard line, they both noticed her at the same time.

"Holy shit! There she is," mouthed Milton under his breath.

She was the girl they ran into on the way out of the O last week. Her long, shiny black hair was a great contrast to her bright red sweater. A sweater that accentuated her enticing figure. She was sitting just two rows down and three seats to the right. When she turned around, they could see her matching red lipstick perfectly drawn on voluptuous lips. Her high cheekbones had a hint of blush, and her smile showed off perfectly aligned, brilliant white teeth.

"I thought you would have already gone out with her," chuckled Chris.

"Give me a couple of weeks and we'll be discussing baby names."

"Actually, I think I am more her type."

"What makes you think that?"

"Well, first she looks intelligent, which means she would be looking to be with someone matching her intellect. And second, I think she just winked at me."

"Dream on poor boy, dream on. I am sure she is looking for someone with lots of money and important connections. And that my friend is exactly me."

"Well, we'll just have to see how things work out. Maybe a small bet would be in order."

"It would have to be a small bet to make sure I can collect!"

"Okay, dinner and drinks at the O for the first one who dates her."

"You're on," Milton agreed as the opening kickoff took place.

As usual, Notre Dame won and a large group of students decided to drown their sorrows at the O. Milton and Chris were among them. The bar was even more crowded than usual, but they were able to find a bar table and were soon joined by Milton's friends from the other night.

"If it weren't for that bad call in the third quarter we might have won," complained Tyler.

Everyone knew Tyler. He was a star on Stanford's baseball team. He was 6'4" tall and could throw a 98 mile an hour fastball. Everyone expected he would skip his senior year and go high in next year's draft. Like Chris, he was from a small Midwest town. In his case, his scholarship was for his athleticism, not his brains. But because of their similar backgrounds, Chris and he immediately hit it off.

"Well guess who just walked in?" whispered Milton.

They all glanced over quickly and saw the more than hot girl in the tight red sweater glide through the entrance. She moved effortlessly through the crowd, but not inconspicuously, since almost every male could be caught staring as she walked by. She headed toward the bar and then took a right turn when she seemed to notice someone in the crowd.

This sudden turn sent her right at Milton, Chris, and their friends. They all straightened up a bit as she neared their table.

"Hi, Chris," she yelled over the crowd as she neared the table.

"Hey Susan, how are you?" Chris replied as Milton's jaw dropped about three inches. "Let me introduce you to my friends."

Chris introduced everyone around before Susan said she was meeting some girls and needed to excuse herself. "I guess I'll see you Wednesday night, Chris," she added.

"Sure, I'll pick you up at 7."

"Perfect, I'll see you then."

After she was out of earshot, the gang started their interrogation. "Where did you meet her?" asked Tyler.

"She just joined my chemistry class."

"That's not fair," chimed in Milton. "You made that bet and you already had a date with her set up."

"Everything's fair in love and war. I guess I'm having prime rib tonight."

CHAPTER 3

Three Years Later

Milton Simon for student body president was the message on a slick banner hanging from the Toyon Lounge. The 500-capacity lounge was more than what was necessary for Milton's campaign meeting, but he could always hope more people would show up. The lounge gave priority to residents of Toyon Hall. Milton lived off campus, but a couple of his friends still lived at the dorm and helped arrange the meeting.

It was just shy of six at night when students began to ramble in, most wearing sweaters or jackets on the cool fall evening. Daylight savings hadn't ended yet, but the sun had almost set, casting long shadows of the tall trees nearby. The beautiful autumn leaves had begun to fall, leaving the ground looking like a patchwork of colored carpet.

Chris was one of the first attendees. "I always knew you would be a politician."

"And I always knew you would end up marrying Susan."

"Too bad she doesn't know that yet."

"Oh, I'm sure she knows. You guys have been inseparable since that first Stanford/Notre Dame game. I never had a chance."

"Well, you have a better chance of becoming the next student body president."

They continued their conversation as about fifty others wandered in. There was plenty of seating on soft, leather tufted couches. A grand piano graced the corner of the room. Some refreshments had been set up on the left side away from most of the furnishings. The 25-foot-high ceiling boasting six wrought iron chandeliers gave the room a majestic feel. A microphone had been placed on a small podium close to the piano.

Milton didn't want to wait too long, since he knew they all had better things to do. At about 6:15 he approached the mike and asked for everyone's attention. The guests finished their conversations, grabbed some refreshments, and found places to sit.

"First of all, I want to thank you all for taking time out of your busy schedules to come here tonight. Many of you have been good friends for our three years here at Stanford. But some I am meeting for the first time tonight, and I especially want to thank you for your time.

I hope you will stay for a little while after this brief presentation so I can greet you personally.

"As you all know, I am running for student body president. It was not an easy decision to start this campaign. But thanks to the encouragement of many of you here tonight, I decided to throw my hat in the proverbial ring. Stanford has meant a lot to me for these past three years and I am the third generation of my family to attend here. So I thought it was time to serve the university. My platform is simple – "A" grades for everyone, more student lounges serving free beer and free football game tickets for everyone who votes for me!"

That created a chuckle from the attendees.

"Just kidding."

"And I was about to vote for you!" shouted one of the students from the back of the room as a chorus of laughter followed.

"Seriously, I do have some ideas on how to make our university better. Recently, we have had outside speakers who expressed some extreme ideology. To curb that practice we should establish a student committee to review and approve any outside speakers. Requests should be submitted at least 30 days before the planned event to give the committee adequate time to research the application. This will help students from being indoctrinated with inappropriate ideologies.

"Second, we need to encourage the administration to accept more minority applications for enrollment at our university. For much too long, minorities, especially our African American bothers and sisters, have suffered unequal treatment, and it's time to take steps to make up for that inequality.

"Third, we should have student representation at board of regent meetings. Students should have a say in how our universities are run. These are a few of my ideas. My main point is, my desire is to represent you, the students at Stanford University.

"Are there any questions?"

Chris, following through on Milton's previous suggestion asked, "What can we do to help you get elected?"

"Thanks for asking," Milton replied with a smile. "Please take some of these posters, buttons, brochures, and bumper stickers and place them wherever you can. Name recognition is what wins elections these days. And don't forget to ask your friends to vote for Milton. Thanks for coming everyone, and enjoy the refreshments."

For the next half hour or so, Milton mingled with those who hung around for the free food. Afterwards Milton invited Chris and a few others back to his off-campus apartment to watch the second half of Monday night football.

On the way, one of the invitees questioned Milton. "I never knew you were so supportive of minority inclusion. When did that happen?"

"When I decided to run for President. Seven percent of the current student body is black, and every vote counts," he replied. "Of course, that's between you and me."

Milton lived at Avalon Towers on the Peninsula. It was where you would expect Milton to reside. A first-class apartment community completely self-contained with its own swimming pool, Jacuzzis, picnic area with barbeques, a recreation room with pool tables and ping pong tables, and a gourmet coffee shop. Milton's apartment had a clear view of the Santa Cruz mountains.

On the way they ordered pizza and stopped at the local 7Eleven to pick up a case of beer, for what was football without pizza and beer? When they arrived, Milton's roommate, Steve, was already watching the game. The Forty-niners were playing the LA Rams. It was an important inter-division game, since both teams were vying for playoff spots.

"I should have picked a different night for my meeting. If it wasn't for this damn game, I would have had a lot more people show up."

"You should have rented a projector and played the game on a big screen. Then you would have had a lot more attendance," chuckled Steve.

"Actually, that would have been a good idea. Your suggestions would be much better if they were provided on a timely basis."

Everyone settled in to watch the Rams win the game with a last second field goal. Not a happy result for the hometown fans. After everyone else left, Chris offered to help clean up the empty pizza boxes, paper plates, and beer cans. Milton declined his offer and explained the maid was coming tomorrow, she would clean everything up.

"It must be nice to live in an amazing off-campus apartment with a maid."

"It's not bad."

"So, how do you think your LSAT went?" asked Chris.

"I'm not sure. I had some problems with a few of the sections, but overall, I think I did well enough to get into law school. How's your research coming?"

"It's incredibly interesting. We are now looking into how to transfer nucleic acids into living cells in order to treat diseases. Several years ago, Dr. Martin Cline modified human DNA using this technique.

We're doing further research to ensure this can be safely used."

"I didn't understand a thing you just said, but it's amazing how fast medicine is improving."

"I don't think we have seen anything yet. In twenty or thirty years we will know enough about the human body to develop treatments for most diseases and prolong life for decades."

"You mean I'll live to be a hundred?"

"Maybe more, if you don't die in a car accident!"

"Well, if you find a way to keep people from getting sick, I better tell my Dad to sell his pharmaceutical company stocks."

"If technology and science keep advancing at this pace, there are a lot of stocks your Dad should sell."

CHAPTER 4

There were simultaneous explosions in university labs across the country. At least seven labs were totally destroyed. All the major news outlets were covering the events. The cable networks were running twenty-four-hour coverage.

The biology and chemistry labs at Stanford, MIT, Harvard, Princeton, UCLA, University of Michigan, and Berkeley were among those targeted. Six people were killed and dozens were injured during the attacks which took place in the early morning hours.

Stacy Ogden was at the right place at the right time.

This was Stacy's first big story since she joined the Times from a small mid-west newspaper. She grew up in Lima, Ohio, a small city near the western border not too far from Fort Wayne, Indiana. She was the editor of her high school newspaper and went on to study journalism at the University of Minnesota. Stacy was average in most ways - five foot five, slender figure, brown hair, green eyes, not particularly attractive, but not totally unappealing to the eyes. But Stacy was smart. She earned a full college scholarship, which was important since her parents couldn't afford to send her to any place other than a community college. And she was intent on becoming a top-notch investigative reporter.

Straight out of college, she returned home to Lima and was hired at *The Lima News*, the local paper in her hometown. After spending a few years reporting on mostly mundane stories, she uncovered a drug ring operating out of her county, which had ties to the local police. It was the biggest story to come out of Lima in decades. Ten individuals, including three police officers, were convicted and sentenced to many years in prison.

This story was her ticket to the big time. Within months of breaking the story, Stacy's application to the *New York Times* was accepted. It didn't take long for her superiors to discover her abilities and how thorough her reporting was. In her first two years, she ran down every lead with the ferociousness of a wild dog chasing its next meal. Her attention to detail was almost insane.

Stacy was visiting her parents over the Thanksgiving holiday when the lab explosions occurred. Since she was so close to Purdue University in Fort Wayne, she volunteered to investigate the explosion there. Her boss was happy to oblige her, since they had no other reporters even close to Indiana. So, after renting a Chevy Malibu from the local Avis office, she set out on the two-hour drive to Fort Wayne.

She drove straight to the university and found a large group of students eulogizing their lost friends. Two students had succumbed to the blast, and six others were severely injured. They were all working late on some important research that was just getting some real traction. The explosion had occurred at one in the morning the day after Thanksgiving. She spent a few hours mingling with the grieving students, trying to get some background. She took some notes from their comments and wrote down a few names and contact information from some of those who worked on the same research projects as those that had died or were injured.

The police had barricaded the labs so, even with her press identification, she couldn't get close to the explosion site. She decided to go to the police headquarters for an official update. The headquarters were housed in the Rousseau Center at One East Main Street. After going through security, she was directed to the information officer. The sign on the door read Jason Miller. Stacy entered without knocking.

Behind the desk sat a middle-aged, balding gentleman who was talking on his telephone when she entered.

"Yes, I know you want more information and when we get it I will let you know." After a pause to listen to his caller, "There is nothing new to report. I must go now, someone just came into my office... yes, I will get back to you if something new becomes available. Bye."

"I guess the explosion has made life a little more hectic."

"Just a little... and I suppose you are..."

"Yes, I am. Stacy Ogden, *New York Times*."

"A little far from home, aren't you?"

"Actually, not far at all. I was visiting my family in Lima when all this happened. Since I was only a couple of hours away, they sent me to investigate."

"Well, I don't have too much for you other than what you probably already know. The explosion took place at 1 a.m. yesterday and killed or injured several students who were working at the lab late. The first indications are that the bomb had a timer and used C-4 as the explosive material. There are currently no leads."

"Can you give me the name of the lead investigator?"

"Sure, it's detective George Menke. He's been with the force for over twenty years. A hometown boy."

"I assume he's at the site now."

"Probably, but I don't keep track of his movements." As he finished the sentence a young man ran into the office.

"Did you hear what they just found? Someone left a note. It's really some kind of manifesto and takes credit for the bombings. It says a group called 'Save Our Babies' is responsible."

"Do you have a copy for me?" Jason asked.

"They're making copies now. I'll get one right to you."

"Can you get one for me, too?"

The young man looked over at his boss for direction. After a pause and looking at her begging eyes, he replied, "Okay, get her one, too."

When the young man hustled out he turned to Stacy.

"You'll owe me dinner for this. This will be a big scoop for you."

"Breakfast lunch and dinner at your choice of restaurant."

She could expense it all with this scoop on all the national media. A few minutes later the young man returned with two copies that he handed to his boss. As he handed a copy to Stacy he said, "I'm going to hold you to your promise – dinner at the Baker Street Steakhouse."

24

"Absolutely, you're on. I'll get back to you shortly, but I have to run and file this story."

Since the *Times* didn't have a bureau office in Fort Wayne, Stacy checked into the closest hotel for some privacy.

She hammered out her story on her laptop, but she still had reservations and a gut feeling that something was off. She couldn't understand why an organization that promoted the sanctity of life would take some. But she couldn't miss the deadline so an hour later she pressed "send" and her byline was off to her editor.

Four hours later her front-page story hit the news with the headline, "Pro-Life Extremists Take Credit for Lab Bombings." The story catalogued all the labs that had been bombed and the damage incurred, as well as the injuries and fatalities. It discussed the manifesto that was found at Purdue, with a copy pictured next to the article.

The line of limos was unusual in Napa. One by one they drove down the center of town and dropped one passenger each in front of the famous French Laundry restaurant. Eight limos in all. Once all of the well-dressed guests arrived and were seated in the private dining room, the gentleman at the head of the table stood.

"I thought we agreed that there would be no human casualties!"

THE PROCEDURE

CHAPTER 5

2022

As they rolled the stretcher toward a private room in the emergency area, the attending physician asked Mrs. Simon some questions.

"When was the last time your husband had anything to eat or drink? Is he allergic to any medications? Has he had any other symptoms lately?"

Although completely hysterical by now, she stammered her answers. Then, as they approached the double doors, the attending told her she would have to remain behind. She did not take that instruction well and had to be pulled away by one of the orderlies. As they were moving through the door, she screamed again, "He shouldn't be sick, he had The Procedure!"

The Secretary was wheeled into the private room and hooked up to several monitors. All his vitals were off the charts. His blood pressure registered 190/120. His heart rate was eighty-five and his EKG was irregular. He continued to have difficulty breathing, even though an oxygen mask was in place to aid it.

"I want a complete blood panel, a urinalysis and send him up for a full body scan," the doctor said.

"We need to find out what is causing this quickly, before he expires."

As he finished with his instructions, another doctor rushed in.

"I understand you have a patient with unusual symptoms."

We definitely do. Why?"

"I just received a report that there are several other patients at other hospitals with the same symptoms. Nobody can figure out what is causing their problems."

Secretary Simon was trying to get their attention. Finally he ripped the oxygen mask from his face and as loudly as he could muttered,

"You have to find Dr. Chris Cummings."

CHAPTER 6

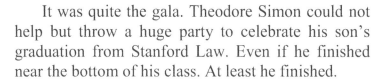

It was quite the gala. Theodore Simon could not help but throw a huge party to celebrate his son's graduation from Stanford Law. Even if he finished near the bottom of his class. At least he finished.

Chris' celebration was quite different. He had flown back home for a nice family dinner at a local restaurant. But his parents were equally proud of his achieving a PhD in both chemistry and biology in record time. His dissertation on gene therapy was applauded by all his professors. It was a short visit because he had to return to Silicon Valley for job interviews. And, of course, to attend Milton's grandiose affair.

"Well, what do you think?" asked Milton.

Chris replied," I think you have a very proud father."

"You would have thought I graduated first in my class."

"You didn't?"

"Ha ha, very funny."

"I assume you have some excellent job interviews coming up?"

"Of course, Dad has arranged a couple of meetings, but he's pushing me to Madison Walsh because they are very politically connected. He's probably promised them a lot of new business if they hire me."

"Interesting. My Dad has set up an appointment for me to meet with Pfizer."

"Really?"

"Of course, not. My Dad's most important contact is the local sheriff."

"Well, I doubt you need any help from anybody to land a great job. You were at the top of your class in both undergraduate and graduate school. Who wouldn't want to hire you?"

"We'll see."

"By the way, where's your wife?"

"Probably discussing the good old days with her girlfriends."

"Ah, the good ole days, when I cajoled you to visit the O occasionally, dragging you away from your studies."

"And you were the prestigious president of the Stanford University student body."

30

"I don't know how I ever won that election."

"As I remember it was a landslide, you won by nine votes."

"Yes, but you won Susan. That was a much bigger prize."

"You're right there, buddy. I found a true life partner."

As the boys were reminiscing, Milton's dad noticed the two and walked toward them. It took him a few minutes to get through the crowd, stopping briefly to smile and shake hands as he made his way to the young men. Theodore was much taller than Milton. His thick gray, almost silver hair draped a chiseled face. He strode with confidence. As he approached, he held out his hand to Chris.

"Congratulations, Chris. I understand you graduated first in your class."

"Thank you, sir."

"Please Chris, call me Ted."

"Yes sir... I mean Ted."

"I'm sure you have many opportunities in front of you. Are you going to take a little break before jumping on life's treadmill?"

"Yes sir... Ted, Susan and I are going to take the honeymoon we never had. We're going to Hawaii for a week. We're going to spend what we hope are small signing bonuses when we get back."

"Chris, don't worry about the cost. I have a friend who owns one of the best resorts in Hawaii. He can put you up and cover all your expenses while you're there. Just give me the dates and I will arrange it."

"I couldn't accept that."

"Of course you can. This friend owes me a favor and I've been trying to figure out how to collect. This helps us both since my friend is feeling an obligation and this way, he eliminates it."

"I don't know, it seems a little much to accept."

"Chris... you have been a good friend to this family and my son throughout college. It's just a token of my appreciation for keeping Milton out of jail!"

"Well, if you put it that way. That was quite a challenge."

"Okay guys, enough of the lovefest. Let's get back to celebrating MY graduation."

"Of course, son, and on that note there is someone I want you to meet. You too, Chris. Meet me in my study in about fifteen minutes."

Ted wandered off without waiting for a response. He climbed the stairs leading from the backyard garden to the rear entrance of the house. Mansion was probably a better term. The 7,000-square-foot home was situated on over an acre of land. The house was built over 50 years ago, but it had been renovated several times since then. Ted Simon bought it fifteen years ago after his first big Wall Street bonus.

Soon after, he went out on his own and started a hedge fund. The combination of making great returns for large investors and raising cash for entrepreneurs in Silicon Valley provided him an endless list of important contacts, all who owed him favors.

On his way to the study, he grabbed two of those contacts. The first was Albert Stein. Albert was the son of immigrants from Poland. He was a rotund man with a deeply receding hairline. You would never guess he was the Chairman and CEO of one of the world's largest pharmaceutical companies. The second was his polar opposite. He was tall and fit. He had the most engaging smile with deep dimples, which made him even more attractive to the fairer sex. All of which was important in his profession – the Senator from the great state of California.

The gentlemen reached the stately office. It was more like a library. Twenty-foot-high ceilings with bookshelves rising all the way up on three sides. Behind a huge mahogany desk on the fourth side were large windows peering out on the immense backyard. There was a fully stocked bar in one corner and a large oriental rug covering a good portion of the polished Brazilian cherrywood floor.

"Can I get you gentlemen something to drink?"

"Yes, I'll take a Maker's Mark, neat," Albert requested.

"I'm fine," replied Senator Billings.

As Ted served himself and Albert their drinks he said, "Okay what is the plan?"

"As you know, California is a very liberal state, so it will be difficult for me to lead the charge. However, of course, we have conservative colleagues from other states who will do the heavy lifting. I will only be able to put up a weak challenge, and in the end use some horse trading as an excuse to go along."

"I understand, but you are confident that we can count on our conservative, and highly contributed to, colleagues?" asked Albert.

"That will not be a problem. This will appeal to their base anyway. In fact, this will be a big win for them and ensure their reelection. And, as you well know, that is the number one priority for everyone in Washington."

"Sounds like a good plan to me," added Ted.

"So let's talk about these boys. I know my son is not the brightest candle in the room, but that will make it easier to control him, and he does have a flair for politics. After all, he did win his only election so far."

"The more allies we have, the better," chimed in Albert.

"So we need to carefully groom him," continued Ted.

"First, we need to get him established in a politically connected law firm. Then we need to help bring in new clients to the firm to raise his visibility there. Eventually, we will find the right time and place to start his political activity. The sooner the better."

"I think you're right and I will arrange the interview with Madison Walsh. Getting him a position there will not be difficult," said the Senator.

"Now there's his friend, Chris, we need to discuss," added Ted.

"He could end up being an asset or a liability. He is a very bright boy and one of a few who could actually end up developing something important in this field. His dissertation was enthusiastically received by his professors and his innovative thinking in the gene therapy area may ultimately produce results. He really thinks outside the box. But he is very independent. On our team he could be a real asset, but on his own he could cause us problems."

"How do we make sure he ends up on the right team?" asked Albert.

"That's where you come in. You should offer him a research job. One so lucrative he can't turn it down. That way you can watch him, and of course, benefit directly from his research. You know what they say – keep your friends close and your potential enemies closer."

"What enemies?" asked Milton as the boys entered.

"Anyone who would try to keep you boys from having an enormously successful life. And I can assure you these two distinguished gentlemen do not fall into that category," added Ted.

"Let me introduce you. This is Albert Stein. As you may know, Albert is the Chairman and CEO of Trident Pharmaceuticals."

"Of course, Mr. Stein, I'm well aware of your company," said Chris as he shook his hand. Milton did not know of him or his company, but he stood forward and shook his hand.

"A pleasure to meet you sir."

"And I'm sure you all know Senator Mark Billings."

"Of course we do," said Milton as he reached out to shake his hand.

"It's a pleasure to meet you sir," added Chris.

"While we were waiting for you two, we were discussing your futures. We all believe that two fine young men like you have endless possibilities ahead. The key will be choosing the right path. And in that regard I have some good news. First, Milton, Senator Billings has agreed to support your acceptance by Madison Walsh. His endorsement will mean a lot. And Chris, Mr. Stein would like you to interview for a senior research position at Trident."

"That is amazing. I'm not sure on short notice your team can arrange to meet me. I have several other interviews this week and my wife and I are going to Hawaii in ten days."

"Don't you worry about that, just let me know what day next week you have available and I will make it work. I wouldn't want to lose such a great candidate for our company to someone else. Here is my card. Give me a call to arrange the time."

"Thank you sir, I appreciate the opportunity."

"Okay, now that that's settled, let's get back to the party," suggested Ted.

"I'm for that," chimed in Milton.

On the way out, Stein passed a small piece of paper to Theodore which contained several symbols. "This is our next play."

CHAPTER 7

Four Years Earlier

Since Stacy broke the story, her editor assigned her to be the lead for all the bombing news. For three weeks she traveled around the country to visit all the bomb sites and interviewed anyone related to them, mostly students and professors.

Although no one had been able to find out any information about this so called Save the Babies group, by the time she got west to Stanford the story was dying down. They had discovered several copies of the identical manifesto at several of the school explosion sites. Other than that, there was little new information being discovered.

It was a windy day, not abnormal for northern California. It was that wind that exacerbated the California fires that raged almost every year. Proper forest management was not a high priority for those in charge. Apparently it was more important to avoid cutting down a hundred trees and scrubs than to keep a thousand acres from burning them away.

Stacy arrived at the science building, or at least what was left of it. She went straight to the department head office, identified herself, and asked if there were any students or professors she could interview. The receptionist said she wasn't sure. The building had little activity since the bombing.

"You're welcome to look around," she said.

"Classes have been postponed so you won't be disturbing anybody."

Stacy thanked her and decided she would take a look around. The police tape had been removed a week earlier so there was nothing to stop her from roaming. After a few minutes, she ran into someone rummaging through the wreckage.

"Hello, my name is Stacy Ogden. I'm a reporter from the *New York Times*. Mind if I ask you a few questions?"

"Why not?" he replied.

"Can I have your name please?"

"Chris Cummings."

"I assume you're a student here."

"Yes, I am also a research assistant."

"What are you researching?"

"Well, I was researching gene therapy that could have a profound effect on health and longevity. We, along with a lot of other schools, have made significant progress over the past decade."

39

"That sounds remarkably interesting and potentially valuable. Can you explain a little about that research?"

"I'll try. In order to replicate, viruses introduce their genetic material into the host cell, tricking the host's cellular machinery into using it as blueprints for viral proteins. Retroviruses go a stage further by having their genetic material copied into the genome of the host cell. We attempt to exploit this by substituting a virus's genetic material with therapeutic DNA. We were working with a number of viruses that could be used for human gene therapy, including retroviruses, adenoviruses, herpes simplex, vaccinia, and adeno-associated virus. Like the genetic material in viruses, therapeutic DNA can be designed to simply serve as a temporary blueprint that is degraded naturally to enter the host's genome, becoming a permanent part of the host's DNA in infected cells."

"Can you try that in layman's language?"

"In simple terms, we use a virus's ability to infiltrate cells to carry therapies to fix problem cells which produce many different types of illnesses."

"How close are you to perfecting that approach?"

"We were getting close, but every lab that was collaborating on these therapies was blown to bits."

"But you must have the research backed up."

"Yes and no. Of course, many of the research notes have been saved, but the gene samples, which have taken years to develop, were destroyed. These bombings probably set us back about four to five years."

"As you probably know, an extremist group called Save Our Babies has claimed responsibility for these attacks. But it doesn't sound like your research involved unborn fetuses."

"That's mostly true. There has been some work in that area, but the vast majority of the research deals with viruses and does not involve fetuses at all."

"Sounds like the group that bombed all these labs was misinformed."

"Either they were misinformed or they had another agenda," suggested Chris.

"I've always had a gut feeling that we should be looking somewhere else to explain these bombings. I never understood why a group that professes to believe in the sanctity of life would actually take lives."

"Well, I've read some of your articles and I haven't seen any suggestion of that there," Chris commented.

"It's my job to write the facts, and so far I haven't been able to find anything substantive to support another scenario. But I will keep looking."

"I hope you do. Whoever did this needs to be punished severely."

"No matter how long it takes, I'm going to find the answers."

"Good to hear. By the way, I'm meeting my girlfriend and some friends at the O for lunch. Care to join us?"

"What's the O?"

"Sorry, it's the campus hangout. There may even be some other researchers there you can interview."

"Okay, sounds good. How do I get there?"

Chris gave her directions and they both walked off in different directions to their cars. Stacy felt like she was getting more questions than answers as she continued her investigation. Who would want to destroy such promising research and who could coordinate such simultaneous attacks? Although, the story was fading from the forefront, she sensed this was just the beginning.

They both arrived at the O parking lot at about the same time. Chris waited for Stacy so he could bring her inside to meet Susan and the others. He held the door open for her as they entered, and he directed her over to Susan's table.

"Hey everybody, I want you to meet Stacy, she is a reporter from the *New York Times* and is here investigating the bombings." Everyone introduced themselves to Stacy as they grabbed a seat.

"Susan, are you a researcher, too?" asked Stacy.

"No. I'm pre-med. But I obviously take some classes in the biology department."

"Have you decided on a specialty?"

"Not yet, but I'm leaning toward internal medicine."

"With your background you must be excited about Chris' research."

"Very much. We discuss it all the time. Chris is very humble so I'm guessing he didn't share with you how integral his work has been to the project."

"You're right, he made it sound like he was just an assistant."

"Sounds like Chris," Milton said as he arrived, late again. "And who, may I ask, is our new friend?"

"This is Stacy, a reporter from the *New York Times*," Susan replied.

"Oh, is she here to interview the new president of the Stanford University student body?"

"No!" everyone chimed in together.

"Then what would a *New York Times* reporter be doing here?"

"I'm investigating the bombings. And Chris was kind enough to give me some good background and then invite me to join you guys for lunch. He said there might be others here who I could interview."

"Well, I'm sure he didn't mean me, since the closest I get to science is political science."

"Stacy is beginning to wonder if the bombings were really orchestrated by this pro-life extremist group," Chris added.

"My Dad said he thinks it was just such a group. According to him these people are a bunch of crazies who will do anything to stop this type of research," said Milton.

"It's hard to believe a bunch of crazies, as you put it, could pull off such a coordinated attack," Stacy replied.

"Maybe I could speak with your dad and get his take on this."

"I doubt it, my dad stays pretty much under the radar."

"Well, here's my card if he wants to talk."

They all ordered lunch and when they were finished eating Chris introduced Stacy to a couple of other research assistants.

Chris and the others left and Stacy remained behind to talk to the other researchers.

Nobody noticed the young man wearing a Giants baseball cap peering intently over his newspaper.

CHAPTER 8

"It's about time you took me on a honeymoon," chided Susan.

"Well, when were we going to have time before? I can't even believe they let you out of your residency for a week."

"Me neither, so let's enjoy the time since it will probably be years before it happens again."

They laid back in their seats as the United Airlines jetliner took off from SFO. Since they made the booking early they were fortunate enough to get bulkhead seats. This was at a time before the airlines realized they could make more money by charging people extra for the "good" seats. It was a four-and-a-half-hour flight to Honolulu and then they would have to switch planes for a short hop to the Big Island of Hawaii. It was back in a time when airlines actually served you lunch. The pretty Hawaiian flight attendants were dressed in Aloha dresses and served tropical drinks to the excited passengers.

As soon as they disembarked in Honolulu the sweet aroma of Hawaii was evident. Purple and pink bougainvillea graced some of the outer walls. The sights and smells were intoxicating. As they passed through the open-air concourse to their next flight, they stopped briefly to visit one of the little shops selling Hawaiian souvenirs and fresh pineapples which could be shipped to your final destination. They decided to splurge and buy some expensive chocolate covered macadamia nuts. They finally found the shuttle that took them to the inter-island terminal.

It was about a 45-minute flight to the Big Island. On approach all you could see was a moonscape of black lava rock with some occasional bougainvillea sprouting from among it. First time visitors began to wonder if they had made the right choice. From the airplane it didn't exactly look like paradise. Even after renting a Mustang convertible and heading south, it was a while before they saw signs that they had not landed on a desolate planet somewhere. After about thirty minutes they saw the signs for Mauna Lani.

They made a left turn into the property and drove through the private road which led to the beachside resort. The road was lined with large palm trees and beautiful flowers and vegetation. When they arrived at the entrance they were greeted by a beautiful Hawaiian girl who placed a sweet-smelling lei on each of them while giving them a double cheek kiss. The gentleman accompanying her handed them a glass of fruit punch and directed them to the front desk where they were asked for their identification.

"Mr. and Mrs. Cummings, so nice to have you join us. Mr. Nakamura wanted to send you his personal greetings," said the front desk clerk.

"Mr. Nakumara?"

"Sorry, I assumed you knew he is our owner. And he has asked me to upgrade you to an ocean front suite for the duration of your visit. We hope you enjoy it."

As Chris held out his credit card the desk clerk said, "that won't be necessary, everything during your visit will be complimentary." Chris and Susan looked at each other sheepishly. They weren't used to this type of treatment.

"Hoolae will escort you to your room. If there is anything you need, please don't hesitate to call me. Oh, and let me know what time you would like to eat dinner tonight. We have reserved a nice table for you at our ocean front restaurant."

"Thank you so much. We're looking forward to our stay at your beautiful hotel."

Hoolae had gathered their luggage and directed them down the winding path toward the ocean front section of the hotel. The hotel was shaped like an arrow. There was an open corridor down the middle with rooms on both sides which led to the "arrow-head" shaped part where the ocean front rooms awaited the fortunate guests. They took an elevator up to the top floor – the fourth.

"This way," he motioned. They took a right out of the elevator and walked just two rooms down to number 402. When Chris and Susan walked in they almost had to hold on to each other. The suite must have been at least a thousand square feet with huge sliding glass doors which opened to an immense balcony overlooking the Pacific Ocean.

"Will this be satisfactory?"

"Are you sure you don't have something a little nicer?" Chris joked, as Susan punched him.

"This will be wonderful. Thank you so much," Susan added.

Hoolae showed them around the room and then placed their luggage on racks. "Will there be anything else now?"

"No, I think everything is just perfect," said Chris. Susan had to give him another punch. "Oh... wait just a minute," as he reached in his pocket for a tip,

"thanks again," as he handed him a ten-dollar bill.

"Mahalo."

Once Hoolae let himself out they first noticed a fresh, tropical fruit bowl on the dining room table and the silver champagne bucket next to it. On closer inspection they discovered it was a bottle of Dom Perignon. Next to it was a card which read –

"Hope you enjoy your belated honeymoon" it was signed Albert Stein.

"Who is Albert Stein?" asked Susan.

"He is the president and CEO of Trident Pharmaceuticals. Remember I interviewed with his company last week. I met him at Milton's graduation party."

"How did he even know we were staying here and that this was our belated honeymoon?"

"I'm not sure, maybe Milton's father told him."

"Why would he do something like this, you hardly know him?"

"I think he's trying to influence my decision to work for their company."

"I didn't know you had an offer."

"I was waiting until I received responses from all my interviews and then thought we could discuss them while we were relaxing out here. Let's just enjoy ourselves for a few days and then we can talk about the future."

"Okay with me. So when are you going to pop that cork?"

Chris took the not-so-subtle hint and poured them both a glass of champagne. After three glasses each, they fell into each other's arms and began to enjoy the intimacy that had been somewhat lacking with both of their busy schedules. He missed touching her soft lips and enjoyed her smooth body pressing against his. They embraced each other tightly, as if for the first time. Their rhythmic hard breathing seemed in harmony with the rolling waves crashing against the beach far below. Their two bodies pressed hard against each other, becoming one, both in mind and spirit.

As their passion continued unabated, she rolled him over and assumed a position on top of his strong body. Her silky, long hair draped in front, hiding just a portion of her well-endowed figure. The surrender to her control and the vision of her beauty looking down at him brought him quickly to a crescendo as he climaxed without notice.

"You didn't wait for me," she complained.

"I'm sorry honey, you're just too sexy. I promise after dinner to do better."

"I'm going to hold you to that. By the way, when is dinner?"

The first few days in Hawaii were quite an adventure. The hotel's concierge had set up several activities, whale watching, a helicopter ride to watch an active volcano, deep sea fishing and surfing lessons. They barely had time to relax on the white sandy beach located right behind the hotel. By the fourth day they told the concierge to take a break and let them just take some time to enjoy the tranquil environment.

They did ask for a blanket and a picnic lunch, which they carried with them as they strolled down the beach to an unpopulated area. They spread out the blanket and opened the gourmet picnic basket. The hotel had packed quite the lunch. It was really an assortment of appetizers that were kept cool with a bag of ice placed in the insulated basket.

"This is incredible," Susan exclaimed as she took out one appetizer after the other. There was a tuna poke bowl, lobster cocktail with a spicy tropical cocktail sauce, shrimp ceviche and salmon pate. And, of course, a chilled bottle of Sauvignon Blanc.

"I guess this is how the one percent live," she added.

"One day we will be the one percent," Chris said.

After they demolished the gourmet treats Susan asked,

"Is it time we talk about your job offers?"

"Sure, why not. As you know, I interviewed with four companies. Two relatively small start-ups, one medium-sized company, and of course, Trident. They all have an appeal for different reasons. The start-ups obviously can't provide the short- term financial benefits, but will include stock options which could turn out to be very lucrative. I would also have some say in the direction the company goes. The medium sized company is based very close to where we live. I could actually ride my bike to work. They have offered a good starting salary."

"How much?" Susan interrupted.

"Sixty thousand a year plus benefits."

"That's really nice!"

"Yeah, I think we could cover our bills with that, but the option pool is very limited."

"And what about Trident?"

"One hundred thousand a year with guaranteed ten percent increases each year for the next five years."

"Whoa!"

"I know, the immediate financial benefits are very appealing and I would be working with a very experienced team of scientists. I could learn a lot and we probably pay off your student loans with the signing bonus."

"What signing bonus?"

"If I agreed to a five-year contract they would give me a $60,000 signing bonus."

"You're kidding?"

"I'm not. You're spending your vacation with a very popular man."

"So what are you thinking?"

"I'm very conflicted. The advantages and disadvantages are so varied. It would be nice to have some extra money for a change. But at Trident, I would be a small fish in an exceptionally large pond. The start-ups can't pay that much now, but the options could turn out very lucrative. Of course, they could turn out to be worthless. Grayson Pharm, the medium sized company, provides a little of both and they are located awfully close to us."

"When do you have to make the decision?"

"There's no rush, but we do need to have some money coming in from somewhere. I'm leaning toward one of the start-ups. I know its riskier, but we're young, we can afford to make a mistake."

"I'll support whatever you decide."

CHAPTER 9

Milton was dressed in his finest, a dark blue Brioni suit with a burgundy tie. He walked into the Madison Walsh reception area, a little overwhelmed by its stately appearance. Across from the well-appointed reception desk was a large conference room with floor-to-ceiling windows that looked over the San Francisco Bay. The room was empty, but he could imagine the people who had important meetings in there.

"Can I help you sir?" asked the attractive receptionist.

"Yes, I'm Milton Simon. I'm here for an appointment with Samuel Hart."

"Please have a seat. I'll let him know you are here."

As he took a seat in one of the expensive chairs, he could feel the moisture forming in his armpits. Even though his father had told him the interview was just a formality, he didn't want to screw it up. He knew first impressions were important, and even if the job was assured, his position at the firm was not.

A slender woman with dark red hair pulled back in a bun walked toward him. "Hello, Mr. Simon, I'm Kathy, Mr. Hart's personal assistant. Please follow me." *I would follow her anywhere,* he thought.

Milton followed her down wide hallways paneled in dark woods. They passed several executive offices on the left with views of the bay and three deep cubicles on the right with people busy at work, pounding on their keyboards. At the end of the hallway, in a spacious corner office, Milton was introduced to Mr. Hart.

"Milton, it is a pleasure to meet you," Hart said as he extended his hand.

"Thank you, Mr. Hart, I appreciate your time."

"Please join me over here." Samuel Hart, fiftyish, a little overweight but with an engaging smile, directed him to a round conference table in the corner of the office. They took seats kitty corner to each other.

"I understand you recently graduated from Stanford Law and will be taking the bar next month."

"That's correct sir."

'Well, if you join our firm we have a special internal bar prep course. Our people are exceptionally good at pre-determining the type of questions that will be on each year's exams. In fact, we have never had one person fail the test."

"That's an amazing record." *I hope I'm not the first.*

"Yes it is, and I am confident that we will keep it intact."

"So, Milton, what is your main area of interest in the law?"

"As you probably know from my file, I was a political science major in undergraduate school. So I remain interested in public policy."

"Well, as you probably know, our firm has a large practice in that area. Several elected officials at local, state and national levels are our clients. We also act as lobbyists for a few large companies. Although we spread our political contributions around where we think they will do the most good, we tend to support a more liberal agenda."

"That was my understanding, but I've always wondered why many wealthy successful individuals and companies have a liberal bias when you would think that lower taxes and less regulation would benefit them more."

"Here's what they don't teach you in college. Money is money, but power is power. You can make more money if you have more power. It doesn't matter how much you pay in tax, as long as you control where it goes. And as to regulation, the more complex the regulation, the less new competition you have, since small companies and especially start-ups have difficulty complying."

"I see, that makes sense. Basically, if tax dollars are distributed in a way that they end up coming back to you, it is in your best interest to have higher taxes. And if you use your influence to pass regulations that appear to be implemented to protect the consumer, but really help inhibit new competition, you have used your power to make more money."

"Exactly. You catch on very quickly, Milton. I think you will fit in here very nicely."

They continued their discussion for another thirty minutes before Mr. Hart said he had other things to attend to and that the firm would be getting back to him shortly with their decision. Mr. Hart's assistant appeared right on time as they shook hands and bid each other goodbye. As he walked out, he dreamed of one day occupying one of those windowed executive offices.

CHAPTER 10

The neighborhood was lower middle class. Residents took care of their property as best they could with limited resources. The DC politicians had not spent money to fix the potholes in the Fort Davis Park area of the city. Most of the city's resources went to the wealthier neighborhoods.

A seven-year-old Ford Bronco with over one hundred thousand miles pulled up to the yellow house with green shutters at 58 Grantham Avenue. The twenty-eight-year-old man, who looked much older than his age, got out and walked toward the house. He wouldn't have been noticeable at all if he wasn't wearing a Giants baseball cap, unusual for a town that supported its hometown Nationals.

As he entered the house he ran into Rachel, the nurse who took care of his wife while he was away. "How's she doing?" he asked.

"No real change. She's resting comfortably for now."

"Did we get any new test results back?"

"No, not yet. I did send in another blood sample yesterday but haven't heard anything."

59

"I don't understand how we can send men to the moon. But we can't figure out what is wrong with my wife."

"I know. It's very frustrating, but you can't give up hope."

"Don't worry about that. I'll never stop doing everything I can to make sure she gets well."

CHAPTER 11

Milton and Chris had remained in touch over the years, but they seldom met in person as a consequence of their busy careers. It was now five years after Milton's grandiose law school graduation party when the two met for drinks and dinner. At Milton's suggestion, they met at the Starlight Room. This was an opulent bar on the top floor of the St. Drake Hotel in Union Square. The room featured lots of red velvet and fancy chandeliers and an amazing view of the city. This wouldn't have been Chris' choice, especially on his budget, but Milton said he would pick up the tab. He said he could expense it anyway. Milton always seemed to enjoy spending other people's money.

"Chris, so good to see you," Milton said as they met at the host's desk.

"You too Milton, it's been too long. I haven't been at anything this fancy since your father set us up for that incredible Hawaiian honeymoon."

'This way please, gentlemen," the hostess interrupted as she seated the two men at a window seat. "Nice to see you again, Mr. Simon," she added.

"You come here often, Milton."

"I bring clients here a couple of times a month."

"Must be nice."

"It's not bad. So how is your job coming along?"

"You know how it is with start-ups, especially those that involve long-term research before any revenue begins. We've made some really good progress on some therapies, but our biggest challenge always seems to be fund raising. Until we finish phase three trials its exceedingly difficult to get a lot of interest. Fortunately, we have a few angel investors who have kept us afloat the past few years."

"That's not my side of the business, but maybe someone in our firm could help. I know we have a lot of heavyweight investors as clients."

"That's not my side of the company either, but maybe we could get our colleagues together to discuss the possibilities."

"Sure, send me the contact info for your financial guys and I'll pass it along to my partners."

"Partners?"

"Yes, that's my big news. I was just made a junior partner. The youngest person ever to achieve that at Madison Walsh."

"That's incredible, congratulations. How did you pull that off?"

"At law firms, the most important job is to bring in new clients. With my father's help, of course, I brought in a few whales, as we call them. The revenue generated from these new clients alone increased our firm's revenue by over seven percent."

"That's amazing, Milton. So other than bringing in new clients, have you been working on any interesting cases?"

"The most important project I'm working on actually deals with your area of expertise, to a certain degree. We are trying to get an out-patient prescription drug program implemented as part of Medicare in a way that doesn't have a negative impact on some of our clients. There are so many competing interests and ideologies that the process is particularly challenging."

"Since I'm not much of a political animal, it's hard for me to understand how these interests compete with each other."

"Well, let me give you a 30,000-foot view of the situation. First, the liberals, for the most part Democrats, want to provide the most benefits possible to their constituents. Next, the Republicans want to provide enough benefits to satisfy a core of their constituents, but must attempt to keep the cost down in order satisfy the conservative ideology of the other constituents. Then you have the pharmaceutical industry, which we represent, who want to make sure that any program that allows them to sell more drugs doesn't negatively impact them in another way."

"How could a program that increases the amount of product a company sells negatively impact them?"

"For instance, some of the ideas floating around Washington, in order to keep the cost of a new prescription program down are, one, allowing individuals to buy prescription drugs in Canada or Mexico where they are cheaper and two, allowing the government to centrally administrate the program, which may lead to the regulation of the cost of drugs."

"Why are drugs cheaper in other countries?"

"Basically because other countries regulate the cost of drugs."

"In other words, Americans subsidize the cost of drugs used by citizens of other countries?"

"It's not quite that simple. Pharmaceutical companies, like most companies, will always charge the maximum amount they can, to make the highest profit. That requires them to consider price versus volume. For example, if they can only sell a hundred tablets at a thousand dollars each, but could sell millions for fifty dollars each, they would reduce the price. They have to analyze what the total market will bear."

"So why doesn't our country regulate the price of drugs like others do?"

"That's also a complicated question. First and foremost, and I would never admit this publicly, but politicians, from both parties, receive substantial contributions from the drug companies. Accordingly, they have lots of input into legislation that impacts them."

"That doesn't surprise me."

"But in addition, the current patent law provides developers of new drugs a legal monopoly for many years. Without competition, they can charge whatever they want."

"Why shouldn't they be able to charge what they want for a product they created? Consumers always have the choice not to buy it."

"Well, that's where the different ideologies come in. The conservative view is that what you create is yours and you should be able to do with that what you please. The liberal view is that everyone is entitled to good healthcare at a reasonable cost. Then the conservatives argue that if a drug company can't earn large profits on its successful product developments, they won't have the money or incentive to try and create new ones."

"I guess that makes sense. I mean our small company is attempting to create new therapies. All of us are working eighty-hour weeks, without vacations and while earning truly little in the hopes we can produce a profitable therapy. If there wasn't a chance for a big payday down the road, why would we take the risk and work so hard?"

"You probably wouldn't, and that's why there hasn't been a change in the patent laws."

"But even those patents expire eventually, and then generic drugs can be purchased for much less. So eventually most people have access to those drugs, right?"

"That's true to a certain extent. The problem is that the FDA is the sole authority to grant new drug manufacturers the license to manufacture generic drugs. And that process can be awfully slow, which reduces the competition, even in the generic drug space."

"I see why your work can be challenging."

"Enough about me and my work. What's up with you? Are you guys thinking about starting a family?"

"I'm afraid I have bad news there. Susan recently found out that she cannot have children."

"I'm so sorry to hear that. And you two would have had such beautiful kids."

"Yeah, we're pretty devastated, although at this time were both so busy, we probably would have had to wait awhile anyway. Down the road we may look at adoption."

"That sounds like a good choice. I'm sure you guys will make great parents."

Chris happened to notice the television over the bar, which had a breaking news broadcast showing what looked like an explosion. The chyron at the bottom indicated that two private labs had been bombed in Silicon Valley. He excused himself from the table to try to hear the particulars. When he returned, Milton could see something was amiss.

"What was that all about?" Milton questioned.

"There were just two private labs bombed. A couple of my friends from Stanford worked at one of the labs. I hope they weren't there when the bombs went off."

"Oh, that's terrible. Anyone I would have known?"

"I don't think so, they were in my chemistry classes, and they didn't socialize much."

Since they had finished dinner, Chris decided to skip dessert so he could check on his friends. "You don't mind if I head out now, do you?"

"Not at all, I understand."

"See you soon and thanks for dinner."

CHAPTER 12

When Chris got home, he called his friend Bob Worthington to check on him.

"Bob, this is Chris Cummings. I just heard about the bombing at your lab. Wanted to make sure you were okay."

"I am, but obviously the lab's not."

"How about Deborah?"

"She's fine. Thankfully, no one was at the lab when the bomb went off."

"Glad to hear that. How about your research?"

"Unfortunately, we lost a lot of our research and, of course, all of our samples."

"Same thing happened to us five years ago at Stanford."

"Do you know who was responsible? What have the police said?"

"No information yet. I got a call from a reporter in New York who is investigating, but I don't think she has any information yet."

"Does that reporter work for the *New York Times*?"

"Yes, how did you know?"

"A reporter from the *Times* interviewed me after our bombing. I think her name was Sally or Stacy."

"Yeah, that's the one – Stacy Ogden."

"As I recall, she was a little skeptical about who was responsible for the bombings five years ago. Even though she was the first one to report on the manifesto found at Purdue University, she had some doubts about their participation as well as their actual existence."

"Well, nobody has taken credit for this one yet."

"This kind of thing could certainly scare people away from our type of research. I think that might be their motive. How was your research coming?"

"We were getting really close, but of course, this will set us way back."

"Sorry to hear that. Well, let's stay in touch, and tell Deborah I said hi."

"Will do. Thanks for the call."

Stacy Ogden was never convinced that 'Save Our Babies' was responsible for the original lab bombings. In between all her regular assignments, she still spent time investigating the bombings. So when these new bombings took place, she was the obvious choice to follow this story. The day following the bombings she caught a flight to Lincoln, Nebraska, the site of one of the private labs.

She had to fly through Chicago on Delta to get to Lincoln, the capital of Nebraska. Lincoln was also a college town which was home to the University of Nebraska and several other smaller colleges. The population was about 300,000 in the metro area, and it was a popular destination for retirees as well because of its low cost of living, at least compared to the east and west coast. She hopped into her rental and immediately drove to the local police station.

When she arrived, she was directed to the public information officer, Thomas Jensen. He was a young man with wavy blond hair, blue eyes, a trimmed mustache, and an inviting smile. He stood when she entered and shook her hand. "Please have a seat."

"Thanks for seeing me. My name is Stacy Ogden and I am a reporter for the *New York Times*. I'm here to investigate the lab bombings."

"You got here pretty fast and a long way from New York."

"Well, I was the reporter for the bombings five years ago, so I'm following this in case they are related somehow."

"We haven't much information to share yet. The only thing we know for sure is that the explosive material was C-4."

"That' interesting. That was the same material used in the bombings five years ago. What was the exact time of the explosion?"

"It was exactly two a.m."

"Do you have the names of the people who worked at the lab?"

"Sorry, no. But I can give you the contact information about the owner of the lab. It was privately owned."

"That would be great."

Thomas rifled through his desk to find the information. "Here it is. His name is William Forest and here's his telephone number."

"Thank you. Do you think I could visit the bomb site?"

"I don't know how close you could get, there is still an investigation going on. The FBI arrived early this morning."

"Okay, I'll drive over that way and see what I can find out. Thanks for your help."

"No problem, here's my card. Feel free to call me with any questions."

"Thanks." Stacy took his card and left. She decided to drive to the site next and just see how close she could get. When she arrived there were several police cars and the FBI presence was noticeable. About five individuals were walking around with FBI emblazoned on their windbreakers in bright yellow letters. The whole area had been cordoned off, so she really couldn't see much else.

It was late afternoon, so she decided to find a hotel room, freshen up and then call the lab's owner.

Just before five she called the number Thomas had given her. William answered on the third ring. "Hello."

Hello, my name is Stacy Ogden from the *New York Times.* Is this Mr. Forest?"

"Yes, it is."

I'm here in Lincoln investigating the bombing of your lab. I was wondering if we could meet so I could get some information from you."

"Well, I'm pretty busy right now, as I'm sure you can imagine."

"I won't take much of your time. I can buy you lunch tomorrow. You have to eat anyway."

"I guess that could work. Just meet me at Mable's Diner, it's on Harold Way."

"I'll find it. Is noon okay?"

"Yes, that'll be fine."

"Then I'll see you then. Goodbye."

"Bye."

With nothing else to do for the rest of the day, she decided to find a nice restaurant for drinks and dinner. She deserved it after a long day of travel. The hotel clerk recommended a place called Harvey's Steakhouse, just a five-minute drive from the hotel. He called ahead and made a reservation for her for 7 pm. She arrived early and decided to sit at the bar while she waited. She ordered a Vodka soda with a twist and enjoyed the relaxing feeling the alcohol provided. She never noticed the man wearing a baseball cap who was sitting in the corner occasionally peering over at her.

She sat at the bar for about twenty minutes before being seated for dinner. She ordered more than she could eat. Her eyes were obviously bigger than her stomach, andshe left a good portion on her plate when she left. After paying her bill she drove straight back to the hotel.

The next morning she called her editor to report in and find out if there was anything new reported about the bombing. He said there was nothing new and she reported her slim findings so far. She told him she would report back after her lunch meeting with the lab's owner. She intended to fly to the other lab site after that meeting.

During the morning she reviewed her notes from five years ago on her laptop. She checked out at 11 a.m. and decided to just drive around the city to get a feel for it. She arrived at Mable's a few minutes before noon and grabbed a table for two off in the corner. The café looked like it must have been around since the 50s. It had a row of tables against the front windows which were opposite a long bar with fixed stools. The linoleum floors hadn't been redone for at least fifteen years and showed the scuff marks from the metal chairs. She continued to watch the front door, looking for who might be William Forest.

Right at noon a tall gentleman, wearing jeans, a white shirt and cashmere sports coat walked through the front entrance. He looked around like he was looking for someone, so Stacy raised her hand. "Mr. Forest," she shouted softly. He saw her and walked over to her table.

She stood up to meet him and after sharing pleasantries they both sat down. "Thank you for taking some time to meet me. I'm sure things are quite hectic right now."

"You could say that. So why is the *New York Times* so interested in a lab bombing in a small town like ours?"

"Well, first, we try to have national focus, not just a local one and second, there may be a connection between these bombings and those of five years ago."

"What makes you think that?"

"Nothing specific other than I believe all the bombings were targeted at labs doing similar research. That's what I wanted to talk to you about."

"That sounds a little ominous. What can I tell you?"

The waitress interrupted their conversation to hand them menus. They decided they would order first and then continue.

"I was hoping you could provide me some details about your research, Stacy said after they ordered."

"Obviously, our research is extremely complicated and would be hard for a layperson to understand, so I will try to give you a simple answer. We are a small company and so our research was very targeted. Our objective was to discover a narrow therapeutic application which would then be sold to a larger company which would enhance and expand the application. Basically, we were trying to develop a method to introduce a pre-programmed virus into a person's DNA that could then instruct the person's own DNA to fight off different types of infections."

"That sounds familiar to what the research labs that were bombed five years ago were working on. How far along were you with this process?"

"We were getting really close. Our experiments with rats were showing real promise. I'd say we were within a couple of years of perfecting it for human trials. Of course, this event will push us back at least two years."

"That's terrible. Do you have any idea of who would want to destroy your research?"

"Not a clue. Most research labs collaborate, so it's not like a competitor would do something like this."

"Based on the information we have from these bombings and the ones from five years ago, the only hypothesis is that a professional was involved," Stacy added.

"I sure hope they catch whoever is doing this. They deserve to be hung and stopped."

"Thank goodness no one was hurt or killed in these bombings like last time."

Stacy and William finished their lunch and bid each other goodbye. She thanked him for is time and they agreed to share any news they got with each other. Stacy was off to the airport to catch a flight to San Francisco. The other bombing was in Silicon Valley. She never noticed the same man with a baseball cap at the restaurant last night was sitting three rows behind her on today's flight.

CHAPTER 13

The champagne was flowing freely at Thompson Labs. Chris and his colleagues were celebrating the sale of their company to a large pharmaceutical concern. All their work was finally paying off. Although the acquirer would use their discoveries across their entire platform of drug therapies, Thompson Labs would remain a wholly owned subsidiary to continue their research.

Chris, since he wasn't one of the original founders, was a minority shareholder. Therefore, his part of the windfall wasn't as large as some of the others, but still a nice pot of money. After taxes he would net about six million dollars. That worked out to about a million a year for his services. Time had flown by so fast he didn't realize six years had already passed since he took the job.

And now with adequate funding, all the employees would finally start receiving an appropriate salary. Of course, they also lost their autonomy. New management set up meetings for all of Thompson's employees to discuss the company's future plans and each of their roles going forward. Chris was scheduled for Tuesday at 3 p.m.

"Chris, please come in and have a seat," directed Warren Houseman, vice president of product development.

"Since we acquired your lab, we have been strategizing on how best to assimilate your firm into our overall objectives. Although we are incredibly happy with the results you have achieved with the gene therapies, we think it would be best to change the course of that research into some areas that may produce quicker results."

"But I thought you bought us because of the success we were having in that area."

"That's true, but we see that as a more long-term project. You know, these days, as a public company, shareholders are looking at our quarterly reports and want to see progress."

"So you're going to table our progress for now?"

"That's the current plan, but we have some exciting new ideas for you to work on."

"I'm not sure I'm comfortable with that approach. I joined Thompson because of the research they were working on and that was where my interest lies. Just developing some improved therapies for sinus infections is not my idea of a career path."

"Even your current bosses have signed off on that approach."

"Well, I'm not sure if you know that I was the lead scientist that created the therapies you bought. Maybe you could start a small, new subsidiary that continues this research. I would be happy to run it and would only need a small staff to continue the work."

"I'm afraid that is not going to be possible at this time. We can address that suggestion down the road."

"That is certainly disappointing. I will have to discuss this with my wife and I will get back to you."

"I understand, we do look forward to having you as a part of the team. I look forward to hearing back from you."

Chris stood and left the room. This was not at all what he expected. It sure took the shine from last week's celebration. He decided to take the rest of the day off to think about this turn of events. He went home and poured himself a glass of red wine, while he waited for Susan to arrive home from her office.

By the time Susan arrived Chris had drunken most of the bottle.

"Hey, honey, you started without me?"

"I'm well past started."

"That doesn't sound good. What's the matter?"

"I had that interview with new management today, remember?"

"Oh, right. It didn't go well?"

"Not really. The company plans to shelve our research for now and go in a different direction."

"What… why would they do that? I mean why would they spend all that money to buy the company and them not follow up on your successes?"

"I can't figure it out myself. Maybe they just wanted to buy the talent. I suggested that they start a small subsidiary, with a small staff, to continue our work. I volunteered to run it."

"And?"

"He said they could consider it down the road."

"What did you say?"

"I told him I would have to talk to you about it and would get back to him."

"Well, what are you thinking?"

"I really would like to pursue this research. I genuinely believe that we can achieve remarkable results, given enough time."

"Then I think that's what you should do."

"But that will take a lot of sacrifice. We will have to invest most, if not all, of what we just got from this sale to fund a new company. I also won't be able to take a salary for a while."

"That's okay. I'm making good money and ultimately this will pay off big for us."

"Are you sure? This is a big decision."

"I have total confidence in you. If you say this can work, I'm 100% behind you."

"There is certainly risk, but I won't stop until I have achieved my goals."

"Then it's settled."

The following day, Chris called Mr. Houseman to let him know his decision.

"I've decided to resign and start my own company in order to follow up on my research."

"I'm sorry to hear that," Houseman responded.

"I'll be leaving immediately."

"I should warn you that you will not be able to use any of the research developed at Thompson going forward. We now own that intellectual property. Also, you will not be permitted back in the facility at this point. We will gather your personal belongings and you can pick them up at the front desk when you return your company laptop and any other company materials you may have in your possession."

"That's fine. There are many ways to skin a cat and you can be assured I will find an even better approach for this gene therapy. Fortunately, our lab shared the building blocks of this approach with others, which placed it in the public domain, in order to speed the progress by collaborating with others. That part of our research is available for anyone to use. I will come by tomorrow to pick up my things," he said as he hung up.

Houseman immediately dialed another number.

"I just heard from Cummings. He's resigned and plans on starting his own company to continue the research... yes, I told him, he said a lot of their research is already in the public domain... Okay, I understand."

CHAPTER 14

The banner read *Milton Simon for Congress*. It hung over his campaign office in San Rafael, a small town about 30 miles north of San Francisco. Milton and his wife had moved there shortly after getting married. It was his father's idea, since the congressional seat in the city would never be vacated by Nancy Pelosi. She'd probably stay in Congress until she was 90, he once said.

It was also his father's idea for him to marry Lucy. Lucy Hopkins was the daughter of an oil tycoon transplanted from Texas to California. The family started in the oil business in the 1950s and had made a fortune by the 80s, which Trevor Hopkins magnified over the last thirty years. They were now California royalty, although they maintained a significant oil business in Texas and Oklahoma.

Theodore Simon was influential in helping his son bring Trevor to Madison Walsh. He had worked on several deals with Trevor before and the families ended up spending time together when the Hopkinses moved to California. Their daughter, Lucy, was six years Milton's junior. She was a beautiful young lady with all the social graces. She was blond, although not naturally, and almost five feet eight inches tall. Even wearing shortish heels, she towered over Milton. She attended Berkeley and graduated with a liberal arts degree in English.

Milton and Lucy first met at a Madison Walsh Christmas party. The firm held a lavish holiday party every year for its biggest clients and top lawyers. It was an event you didn't want to miss if invited. Clients flew in from around the world to attend. Of course, the clients wrote off the trip as a business expense to meet with their lawyers. The party was held in the exquisite ballroom of the Fairmont Hotel every year. Dom Perignon flowed freely. Large buffet tables were conveniently set throughout the room holding the most gourmet treats. Everything from huge shrimp cocktail to a caviar station and beef wellington were just a few of the offerings. A twenty-piece orchestra played all night.

The Hopkinses arrived fashionably late with their daughter Lucy. Milton was one of the assigned greeters. When the Hopkinses entered the party, Milton was the first to greet them, especially since he had brought the Hopkinses to the firm. He had never met Lucy before and was obviously enamored with her appearance. She wore a simple black cocktail address which stopped several inches above her knees, showing off her perfectly contoured legs. Her shoulder length blond hair curled around her face and her bright blue eyes were piercing.

"Good evening Mr. Hopkins. I'm so glad you could attend."

"Hello, Milton. Nice to see you. I think you know my wife Brenda and this is my daughter Lucy."

"Yes, nice to see you again, Mrs. Hopkins and very nice to meet you, Lucy."

"Nice to meet you, too," she said as she shook his hand.

"Since you've moved to California now, it's not such a trek to join the festivities here."

"Yes, that's one of the advantages of living here now," replied Trevor.

That was the beginning of a relationship that flourished over the coming years. Milton and Lucy began dating a few months later, once Milton got up the nerve to call her. Two years later they were married in a huge ceremony and wedding party. They took a three-week honeymoon immediately following in Europe.

After the honeymoon, Theodore asked his son to come over to discuss his future. They decided to have dinner at the House of Prime Rib with their wives and then go back to the house for after dinner drinks and a talk. He suggested they bring an overnight bag so they wouldn't have to drive home that late at night.

The House of Prime Rib was a San Francisco staple. They were always busy. The restaurant had a red canopy over its entrance which proudly displayed that they had opened in 1949. The smell alone as you entered was enough to make you hungry. It was famous for carts that wheeled around the room carrying delicious prime rib which was carved to your specifications right in front of you. Then they added their famous Yorkshire pudding and creamed spinach to complete the meal.

Not much of consequence was discussed during dinner. The women chatted about current fashion trends and local gossip, while the men talked about golf and the local sports teams. Milton had driven to his parents' house before dinner and they all took the limo to dinner. As they were finishing dinner, Trevor called his driver to pick them up. The car was waiting as they exited the restaurant.

When they arrived home the men went off to Trevor's elaborate study while the women sojourned to the kitchen. Trevor poured them each a brandy and they sat in the tufted leather armchairs near the fireplace.

"We need to talk about your future, Milton."

"Looks like things are going fine to me. I have a great, well-paying job and a beautiful, intelligent wife."

"That's quite true, Milton, but I think we have to set our sights higher."

"What did you have in mind?"

"I think it's time for you to consider entering public service. You remember I had suggested you move to San Rafael in order to not be in Pelosi's district. Well, the current congressman from your district is retiring next year. This will be the perfect opportunity to start your political career."

"I'm only thirty years old, do you really think I'm ready?"

"Absolutely. And I've already been doing some groundwork. The Party thinks you would make a great candidate."

"Well, I'm open to your guidance, but I really don't have a clue how to get started."

"The first step is to hire a campaign manager and finance chairman. I have two people in mind. Then you start an exploratory committee. You start making speeches at various events and service clubs. Don't worry, I'll be there to guide you through the hoops."

"I assume we need to get started right away. What about my job?"

"You'll go on a sabbatical for now and then resign when you get elected."

"You mean if I get elected."

"You'll get elected. These things are not as random as everyone thinks. With the right people in place, the right support, and enough money, the result is never much in question."

"You're telling me that by this time next year I'm going to be in Congress?"

"That's exactly what I'm telling you. But there is a long road ahead of us, and we must play this right. Next Tuesday I have set up a meeting with your new campaign operators here at the house. On Monday you need to inform your firm about your plans. This will give you time to finish up any projects you're working on or pass them on to others. You'll have to be on the campaign full-time within two months from now."

Milton admired the banner as he entered the campaign office. *Who would ever believe I would be a congressman*, he wondered. The staff had gathered for their regular Monday morning meeting. They discussed the most recent polling results, Milton's upcoming schedule and a few talking points for upcoming press interviews. He had a decent lead in the polls, partially because of not having to deal with a messy primary like his Republican opponent did.

"If we don't make a mistake, this one is in the bag," said Lucas Smith, the campaign's manager. "But we don't want to stop the fundraising. We'll want to finish off the campaign with a big TV blitz. How are we coming with the donations?"

"Just fine," replied the finance chairman. "We should have at least another half million in by next week. In that regard, Milton, don't forget you have that important meeting tonight with your main donors."

"Don't worry, I won't. My father has already reminded me about ten times."

After a full day of speaking and press interviews, Milton drove to a small out-of-the-way restaurant for this important meeting. By the time he arrived, six men had already been in full discussions. He knew two of the men, and of course his father. He greeted those he knew and was introduced to the other three by name, but not profession or title. They had already opened several bottles of expensive wine and Milton was offered his choice.

"The gentleman who appeared to be the leader said, "Why don't we order dinner and then we can begin our meeting." Hearing no objection, he waved the waiter over. Everyone ordered their meals and the waiter left to submit them.

The same gentleman began, "Gentlemen, it appears that we are dining with the next congressman from our district. We are honored to have been a big part in making that happen, and we look forward to working with you going forward."

"Of course, I'd like to thank you all for your support in this endeavor. I owe you a debt of gratitude," Milton added.

"This is just the beginning. And it is important for you to understand that we expect great things from you and for your career in politics to grow substantially. And, of course, you realize that in return for that support and guidance, you will be prepared to help us when necessary in the future."

Milton began to understand the real purpose of this meeting. It was not an early celebration, but a litmus test for his future cooperation.

"Of course, he understands that," Theodore Simon interjected. "Isn't that right Milton?"

"Definitely," Milton quickly added.

"You need to understand that there will be certain government actions or legislation that are important to us, and we will need your help, along with many others like you who we have supported, to make sure the government acts accordingly."

"I understand, one hand washes the other."

"Now that we have a mutual understanding, let's enjoy our dinner."

After dinner they exited the restaurant to waiting limousines. The gentleman who chaired the meeting was first in line.

A thirtyish driver wearing a Giants baseball cap opened his door for him. He ducked into the car and closed the door without a farewell greeting.

CHAPTER 15

Five years had passed since Chris had started his small research lab. He invested most of the windfall he got from Thompson and was able to persuade a few angel investors to put in some capital. He still had majority control of the company, but he was afraid without a breakthrough soon he would have to give up that control. He had worked six days a week, about twelve hours a day. He had a small, dedicated staff, but everyone was getting pretty burned out.

They finally had a breakthrough on one of their research paths. A human HGF plasmid DNA therapy of cardiomyocytes treatment for coronary artery disease looked promising to correct the damage that occurs to the heart after a myocardial infarction. After MI, the myocardium suffers from reperfusion injury which leads to death of cardiomyocytes, consequently reducing proper cardiac function. Transfection of cardiac myocytes with human HGF reduced the ischemic reperfusion injury after MI.

As a result of this breakthrough, the FDA granted them a fast-track designation which permits an expedited review to facilitate development of drugs which treat a serious or life-threatening condition and fill an unmet medical need.

As a result of this success the original angel investors agreed to additional capital support. To maintain control, Chris agreed to accept the additional capital as a loan, which could be converted to equity if certain milestones were not met on a timely basis. With this cash infusion, the company was able to hire additional scientists to speed up their development of several other therapies.

Within six months, another team had advanced a therapy using genetically modified T cells which attacked cells with cancerous CD19 genes on their surface. The therapy allowed patients' immune systems to make normal T cells after a couple of months. A T cell is a type of lymphocyte. T cells are one of the important white blood cells of the immune system and play a central role in the adaptive immune response.

Their success had not gone unnoticed. Several large pharmaceutical companies wanted to purchase the IP. Chris was initially opposed to turning over his research to someone else, but eventually his investors persuaded him that a sale of the IP would bring in enough cash to sustain the company, pay off the last round of debt financing, and give him enough cash to continue pursuit of his primary research objective. He met with four large companies, including Trident.

After a couple of months of due diligence and negotiations, Chris finally agreed to sell both research area IPs to Trident. Chris met again with Albert Stein at the closing.

"You've done quite well for yourself over these past ten years, Chris," Stein said. "I would have saved twenty-five million if you had agreed to work for us," he continued, as he handed Chris a cashier's check for $25,000,000.

"Thank you, sir, I will put this money to good use."

"And what that might be?"

"That is confidential at this point, and it will not be for sale at any price."

"I guess we'll see about that. Usually everything has a price."

CHAPTER 16

2022

The emergency room was filling up quickly. Nine more patients with similar symptoms to Secretary Simon were being admitted. They were going to have to find another triage area to handle the influx. They were also getting calls from other hospitals nearby and from other cities. It was starting to look like they may have a pandemic on their hands. It was the last thing they needed, having just gotten over the Covid-19 virus a year ago.

Lucy Simon was frantic. She called her father to report what was happening. He said he had heard about this already on the late news at 11 p.m. since he lived on the west coast. The news had not yet reported that Milton was one of those inflicted.

"I don't know what to do," she cried.

"Right now, you just need to settle down. The doctors at Walter Reed are the best in the nation. They will know what to do."

"They don't look like they know what to do. Everyone is running around here like chickens with their heads cut off. It sounds like they have neve seen symptoms like this."

"Just relax, they will figure it out. Do you want me to come be with you?"

"Not right now, it's late there. Let's see what it looks like in the morning."

"Okay, I'll call you when I wake up."

"Bye Dad, and thanks."

Dr. Samuel Reed, no relation, was called in. He was the chief resident at the hospital. "So what do we have here?" he asked Milton's first attending.

"Actually, we have no idea. Secretary Simon and nine others have the same symptoms. They all have high temperatures, high blood pressures, and trouble breathing. We did full body scans on four of them and saw nothing unusual. The blood panels didn't show any viruses nor did nasal swabs. They all look like perfect healthy people who might be dying."

CHAPTER 17

As expected, Milton was elected to serve as the congressman from California's second district. It wasn't even close. He won with 58% of the vote. The entire family and his key campaign staff people watched the returns from his father's house. They waited to open the champagne until he was officially projected the winner and he had received a congratulatory call from his opponent.

"Well son, you are finally on your way."

"It wouldn't have been possible without your help, Dad."

My help, he thought. It was all me. "I was glad to have a small part in your election. Now comes the hard part, representing the people who supported you. I'm sure you will remember who they are."

"Of course. In the meantime I'll have to get started right away to set up my office. I guess I can convert my campaign office into my district office. Then I'll have to hire a staff for here and in

Washington and, of course, get an apartment in DC for Lucy and me."

"Speaking of staff, I have someone I think you should consider for your chief of staff," said Theodore.

"Really, who's that?"

"His name is Bart Kingston. He has served as chief of staff for some other congressman so he can help you learn the ropes."

"I'll look forward to meeting him."

"He'll actually be out here at the end of the week. I'll connect you two by email and you can arrange to meet."

"Okay, thanks Dad."

For the rest of the evening they celebrated victory with the finest wines and a fully catered dinner. By around midnight, everyone was exhausted and began to leave. Milton and Lucy stayed overnight and drove home the next morning.

There was a lot for Milton to do, and he dove right in. He called a realtor in Washington to scout out some potential apartments. He spoke to his campaign office landlord and extended the lease and worked with an architect to convert the space to a district office. Then he began interviewing candidates for staff positions. He only needed a receptionist and one staff member for his local office. He planned on flying to Washington next week to interview people there for the DC office.

The days flew by with all the work and planning and Friday arrived before he knew it. He had emailed Bart Kingston and decided to meet him for lunch to discuss the chief of staff position. He chose the Spinnaker Restaurant in Sausalito. It was an upscale restaurant right on the bay with magnificent views.

It was very expensive, but he could expense everything anyway. *What's a couple hundred dollars out of a multi-trillion-dollar budget.*

Bart was waiting for him when he arrived. Milton saw a well-dressed gentleman in his 50s waiting in the lobby and approached him. Bart stuck out his hand first.

"Congressman Simon, nice to meet you."

"You must be Bart," Milton replied.

"Yes I am. It's a pleasure to meet you."

"That's the first time I have been greeted as Congressman Simon. It does have a nice ring to it."

Bartholomew, Bart for short, was 53 years old. He was a graduate of Harvard and received his master's degree from Cambridge University. He got started in politics right out of school and got an internship in the White House during the Clinton administration. From there he got a job as a junior staff member for one of the Democratic congressmen from Massachusetts. Eventually he ended up as chief of staff for Congressman Waldman, and after his retirement, he was hired by his replacement Congressman Stark. Stark served on the important House Appropriations Committee. He was Chairman of the Subcommittee on Health.

As a result of his employer's position, Bart had significant contact with many participants in the healthcare arena. He met with lobbyists and healthcare companies on a regular basis. Congressman Stark had received substantial support from many of these healthcare players so it was Bart's job to keep them appeased. It was Stark's job to vote for the right legislation. Bart understood the game and knew how to play it.

The hostess sat the gentlemen at a table for two right on the window. The Spinnaker's shoreline location in Sausalito's historic downtown offered them stunning panoramic views. With floor to ceiling glass walls, they had incomparable views of the San Francisco skyline, Angel Island, Belvedere, Alcatraz, the Bay Bridge.

The waiter approached and offered water and suggested a nice white wine to enjoy with a seafood lunch, the restaurant's specialty. Milton accepted his recommendation and the waiter left to get the wine. Upon his return they both ordered a Crab Louis appetizer followed by fresh swordfish, the daily special.

The two spent a couple of hours enjoying lunch and discussing first Bart's past and then what Milton could expect once he got to Washington. It was obvious to Milton that Bart had substantial experience which he could draw on. Before lunch was over, he decided his father had once again made a good recommendation.

"Well, Bart, I think you would make a great Chief of Staff. If you're open to working for a neophyte congressman, I would like you to take that position."

"I welcome the opportunity. There is a lot to do in the next two months to prepare, so I suggest we get started right away."

"Couldn't agree more. Let's meet at my office first thing Monday morning and we'll get started."

"I will see you then," Bart said as the two gentlemen left the restaurant.

Bart let Milton drive off first before he called for his car. A few minutes later a black limousine drove up. The chauffer, wearing a Giants baseball cap, got out and opened the back door for Bart.

CHAPTER 18

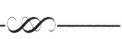

Milton flew to Washington after Christmas with Lucy to set up their new apartment before he was sworn in as a new Congressman on January 3. They had rented an apartment in Georgetown. It was a two-story townhome with three bedrooms and three baths. There was an extra room which Milton planned on using as a home office.

They were so tired from the move that they skipped all the New Year's Eve parties that they were invited to. They figured they had plenty of time to catch up on the DC social life.

On January 3rd, the House of Representatives followed its well-established routine on the opening day of a new Congress. The proceedings included electing and swearing in the Speaker, swearing in members, electing and swearing in house administrative officers, and adopting rules of procedure and various administrative resolutions. Resolutions assigning many members to committees were also be adopted.

The house took these actions at the beginning of each new Congress because it is not a continuing body. Article 1, Section 2 of the Constitution sets a term of office for Members of the House at two years. So every house ends at the conclusion of each two-year Congress, and the newly elected Representatives must constitute a new house at the beginning of each new Congress.

It was a glorious day for Milton and his family. His parents had flown in for the ceremony. It was especially exciting when Milton was the only junior member of Congress appointed to the important House Appropriations Committee. Milton wasn't even sure how that happened, but he wasn't about to go complain about it.

After all the house business was concluded, the Simons went to dinner at the Occidental Grill and Seafood restaurant. For over 110 years the Occidental was a gathering place for the nation's political power brokers, sports figures and celebrities. Milton couldn't help but notice the photos of those notables lining the walls of the restaurant, wondering if one day his picture would be there as well.

"We're so proud of you, son," said his mother. "You are the first person in our family to have attained this honor of serving your country."

"I hope I can live up to that important calling."

"I'm sure you will, son," added Theodore. "Speaking of that, Milton, it is important that you make sure you get appointed to the sub-committee on health. You have plenty of supporters who can benefit from your help there and your background of working on the prescription drug program while at Madison Walsh will be helpful."

"I agree, Dad. That makes a lot of sense. I'll speak to the Committee Chairman first thing."

The group spent the rest of the joyous evening discussing family memories. But Milton couldn't help but notice a striking redhead at the bar who would glance over at him several times during dinner. A couple of times she even seemed to be staring. It was a little uncomfortable, but exhilarating at the same time. When they all got up and left, Milton directed them to the exit so they would pass close by where she was sitting so he could get a closer look. She was even more beautiful up close. She was wearing a low cut red cocktail dress which showed off her well-endowed cleavage. Her long shapely legs were clearly visible since she hiked up her dress while sitting on the bar stool. He wasn't sure if he was imagining it, or did she actually wink at him with her sparkling green eyes as he walked by? He was probably just imagining it, even though his manhood was becoming slightly aroused.

Theodore Simon bid his family goodbye and told his wife he would meet her back at the hotel. He had a meeting to attend with east coast clients who had agreed to meet him in Washington.

"Isn't it a little late for a meeting?" she asked.

"It is, but it was the only time they could meet. They are very busy people."

"Okay, but try not to be too late."

"I won't."

While the others took off for their hotel, Theodore grabbed a different taxi.

"The Jefferson Hotel, please," he requested of the driver.

In the lobby of the Jefferson, three men were waiting for Theodore.

"Sorry I'm late. Dinner went longer than I had expected."

"Understood, it is quite an important day," replied Albert Stein. "And thanks to our friend here, everything we needed was accomplished."

"Well, it wasn't completely my doing. Your well-placed contributions were more than helpful," said Bart Kingston.

"It doesn't matter who takes or deserves the credit, the point is we have our man in place," said the third man.

"Just make sure he now gets appointed to the proper sub-committee. There are a lot of important issues coming up in this session where we will need an ally."

"Don't worry, I have that under control," Bart answered.

"How many friends do we have on the committee now?" Stein questioned.

"With Milton that makes six," Bart responded.

"The more the merrier," added Theodore.

The four men spent the better part of another hour discussing their legislative strategy. As they left their meeting feeling confident about their future, Stein handed Theodore a small piece of paper and said, "tomorrow." Theodore nodded in return as they exited. Instead of leaving with the group, Theodore took the elevator to the fifth floor. He knocked gently on the door of room 505.

The door was opened by a striking redhead, wearing nothing but six-inch black high heels.

CHAPTER 19

She must have had a fantastic orthodontist. Her bright, white teeth were perfectly aligned. Her lips were puffy and moist and glimmered from the red gloss she re-applied when she heard the knock on the door. Her breasts stood up straight, either from her youth or her cosmetic surgeon. But Theodore didn't care which, as he grabbed her to him.

"I thought you'd never get here," the redhead complained.

"I had a meeting I couldn't get out of. They just kept talking."

"The time for talking is over," she said as she began to undress him. His coat was flung on the floor, his shirt was hastily unbuttoned and his pants fell to his ankles. He almost tripped as he shuffled them toward the bed. As he fell to the mattress, she pulled his pants and Jockey shorts off and made her way immediately to his erect penis. He moaned in satisfaction as she caressed him in a way nobody else had ever done. Then she moved her way up and licked his chest as she reached again for his lips. Their tongues played with each other for a few minutes before he rolled her over and penetrated her. He couldn't hold back for long as he exploded inside her in just a few minutes. She hadn't reached an orgasm, but she was used to that with Theodore.

"So what's the deal with your son?" she asked while they embraced after he was finished.

"We just want an insurance policy," he replied.

"Who's the we?"

"You never mind about that. As long as you get paid, it shouldn't matter."

"Well, if I have to have sex with him it's going to cost more." Theodore just laughed.

"What kind of insurance policy? Won't he always do what you say?" she continued.

"Up till now he has, but one day he may grow a pair of his own, and we need to make sure we have the appropriate leverage.

So yes, you are going to have to perform your special services for him. It looked like you set the hook tonight."

"I think I did my job well. I couldn't help noticing his pants got a little tight in the crotch as he walked by. Like father, like son," she added.

"That's a good start. I will keep you posted on his schedule so you can continue to be at the right place at the right time."

"When should I move onto phase two?"

"Let things progress naturally. You'll know when the time is right," he said as he rose from the bed to get dressed.

"You have to go so soon?"

"Yes, Crystal. I have to get back to my wife. Meetings don't go to one in the morning." He finished dressing, reached down and gave her a long kiss goodbye and left the room.

Crystal Devore lay on the bed wondering if this was the life she had planned for. She grew up in Los Angeles, city of angels. Not! More like the city of stars and would-be stars. She was one of the would-be stars. Her acting career never materialized. Her parents, divorced when she was eight years old, provided little guidance or support. So eventually she relied on the one attribute she had – her looks. She was beautiful, even as a little girl.

She matured faster than most of the other girls and was initially embarrassed by her growing breasts, but soon recovered as the boys found them appealing. After high school, with no scholarship or funds for college, she decided to try acting. She had performed in a couple of school plays, but she found getting a professional job much more difficult than she expected. Cattle call after cattle call her less than enthusiastic agent sent her to.

111

She got a couple of minor roles in commercials, a small walk-on for a daytime soap opera, and several extra roles.

You couldn't really call them "roles," she thought. She certainly wasn't making enough money to survive.

Like many others like her, she had to resort to the high-end escort business to make ends meet. It was less degrading than she thought it would be. At the prices the agency charged for her, she only spent time with well-heeled men. They would take her to dinner at places she had never been able to afford. Sometimes they gave her expensive gifts. Several times a year she would go on vacations with her johns. Sometimes she even enjoyed the sex.

Then one day she met a man who wanted her full-time services. Not just for him, but for his business associates, too. In return, he set her up in a plush Westwood condo and paid her two hundred thousand dollars a year in salary. She didn't know for sure, but had an inkling that the apartment had well concealed cameras strategically placed in the bedroom. It was in this apartment that she met Theodore Simon.

CHAPTER 20

With twenty-five million in the bank, Chris was able to hire additional staff and accelerate his research. But this type of research is very laborious and moves very slowly. The initial focus of the research was cellular reprogramming. By introducing a combination of genes into animal cells, the tissue in the cells was rejuvenated, as though they were young again. By healing the cells, they could start new growth, like they were young. They needed to figure out how to deliver that to patients in a safe way, then it was quite possible that aging would be a reversible disease.

After hundreds of experiments, they finally came up with an approach with promise. By using a combination of factors used to make stem cells in a dish, they discovered that they could introduce them into an animal as well. They tolerated it well and tissues rejuvenated. This breakthrough had the whole team reinvigorated. They had gone several years without making significant progress, and hope was now on the horizon.

As their research progress continued, Chris' investors wanted to discuss how to protect their IP.

They arranged a meeting with a notable patent law firm. Chris was always more interested in the science side of the business, but realized protecting their work was important. He and his key investors met with James Jorgensen of Jorgensen, Howell & Hurley to discuss this issue.

Their Silicon Valley office was as impressive as you would expect for a firm that was employed by most of the key high-tech players in the valley. Chris, two of his investors, Jorgensen and two of his associates sat around the large conference table.

"Well, what can we do for you gentlemen?" questioned Jorgensen.

"Our research has begun to show some real progress and my investors and I think it is time to consider ways to protect it."

"Can you tell me a little about your research? Of course, everything you tell me is covered by attorney/client privilege."

"Our basic research involves using a form of gene therapy to increase human longevity by reducing the incidents of disease which causes aging. The ultimate process will involve a combination of drugs, DNA sequencing, and a special process for applying them."

"That sounds amazing. How long will it take to complete your work on this?"

"It's a little hard to say, but our hope is within the next five years."

"Do you know if anyone else using this approach?"

"Of course, you don't know what you don't know, but we have not heard of anybody else heading in this direction."

"First of all, you are right to realize that this kind of research needs protection. If you can accomplish this objective, you will have an unbelievably valuable IP. The first thing we need to consider is whether or not to patent the process. The problem with patents is once you show the world what you are doing, large companies will make minor changes and steal your work. They will make just enough changes to provide themselves a reasonable defense."

"If we can't patent our discoveries, how do we protect ourselves?" Chris asked.

"You can patent them, but you need to understand the risk. Based on what you've told me, I think the best course of action is to keep all your work confidential. This means that even your staff will have to be somewhat kept in the dark."

"They are an integral part of the research. How can I do that?"

"You mentioned that your process involves three distinct areas. Is it possible to segregate your research teams into separate groups, allowing each group to have only limited access to what the other groups are doing?"

Chris thought for a minute and then said, "I think that would be possible, but I'm afraid that may offend our team. We have worked so close and hard on this for years."

"Better to have a few offended than to lose your IP to an unscrupulous company. And don't worry, I will play the bad guy. Just set up a company-wide meeting and I will make a presentation that will alleviate their concerns."

After a little more discussion, they agreed with Jorgensen's suggestion and set the following Wednesday for the employee meeting.

The following Wednesday all of the lab's employees gathered in the open space among the research cubicles. Chris introduced James Jorgensen to the group and turned the meeting over to him.

"Good afternoon everyone. As Chris said, I have been retained by your company to establish protocols to ensure the best possible protection for the amazing research you all are performing here at Cummings Lab. As you probably know, your company works in a very cutthroat space. Any number of individuals or companies would love to get their hands on your hard work. So it is our job, all of our jobs, to do everything possible to ensure that doesn't happen. As I understand, all of you have a lot to gain once this process is commercially available, so everyone has anincentive to make sure it is not stolen. Consequently, we are taking a few steps in that regard.

First, security will be hired to protect the building. Second, the locks are all being changed this evening and an electronic key card will be required to enter or leave. Everyone's coming and going will be monitored and recorded. Third, all employees will be required to sign non-disclosure agreements. At the end of this meeting we will pass them out. You can review them tonight, but they must be signed before you are given a passkey. And lastly, I understand that the process you are working on involves three separate areas. From now on, information about the work of your team will be kept within the team structure and not shared with another team's members unless absolutely necessary. I know these steps may seem a little draconian, and I assure you Chris fought me on every step, but in the end, this is in everyone here's best interest. Are there any questions?"

"Yes, what if we aren't willing to sign the NDA?" asked one of the research scientists.

"Unfortunately, you will have to be terminated. Chris understands some may have a concern about these measures, so he has established a fair termination package for those who decide to leave. Of course, he hopes no one makes that decision, but believes anyone who does should be fairly compensated."

"Any other questions?"

"Hearing none, I'll turn the meeting back over to Chris."

"I know this may come as a surprise to some of you, but many of you have worked for other larger companies that have similar precautions in place. We have now come to a time where it is necessary for us as well. I hope each of you understand and appreciate the steps we are taken to protect us all. I'll be in my office if anyone would like to discuss this further. Thanks everyone. See you tomorrow."

CHAPTER 21

Barack Obama had just been elected on a theme of hope and change. The biggest change proposed in his platform was the passage of a major healthcare plan. Milton Simon, who had risen to the position of Chairman of the Subcommittee on Health, would be a major player in that legislation.

By now, Milton was feeling his oats. Over the past several years he had grown in stature in the Democratic party, mostly through the efforts of his chief of staff and father's contacts. Of course, he had no idea that he was not the sole reason for his ascendence. He had also started a family with two young boys. And privately, he had a robust affair going on with a beautiful redhead.

But helping pass this new healthcare legislation would be his coup d'etat. It would not be an easy task. There were many competing interests and ideologies to consider and appease. Most everyone agreed that healthcare costs were way too high, and that the country needed to find a way for everyone to get coverage, but there were many ideas on how to achieve that.

The far left, of course, wanted a single-payer system like Medicare. The conservatives preferred a non-public approach. Different participants in the healthcare industry wanted to protect their own turf. Insurance companies wanted to preserve their role. And all the politicians wanted to cover their asses so they could get reelected. No, this was not going to be an easy process. In fact, it became one of the most complicated legislative processes in the history of America.

There were multiple stories about this topic airing on all the cable news channels. Congressmen from both sides of the aisles were quizzed on their positions. Senator Haskley, a Republican representing Kansas, was giving his take on CNN.

"We all agree that the main problem in the healthcare space is its rising cost. Today, we spend about 17% of our GDP for healthcare alone. Here are just a few contributors to that problem with some potential solutions. The first contributor is the third-party payer system. Very few people pay for their own healthcare, whether it be those with their own personal insurance, those covered by employer plans, those covered by government plans or those who don't pay at all because they have no money. When someone else foots the bill, there is little incentive to make sure the costs are competitive and appropriate. If you go to dinner and someone else is paying, you order steak and lobster, appetizers, and dessert.

But when you are paying, you order chicken, skip the appetizer, and share a dessert. The same can be said for healthcare – when someone else picks up the bill you don't ask how much it costs, how necessary the procedure and how competitive the price. You just have it done.

You also don't have an incentive to live a healthy lifestyle or take preventative healthcare measures."

"I understand that, but how do you fix it?" questioned the program host.

"The solution can come in many forms, but must address this lack of incentive. You can offer healthcare plans with very high deductibles – which make the insureds responsible for the first dollars spent. You can implement plans that reward individuals who spend less on healthcare by providing them current or deferred rewards. Any plan which produces an incentive to cut costs will result in individuals becoming better healthcare consumers. They will make sure pricing is competitive, they will use more cost-efficient approaches, they will practice preventative care and healthier lifestyles, and they will make sure all services performed are necessary and cost-efficient. And lastly, require all medical providers to disclose all the costs and alternative treatments available upfront, so consumers are completely informed before making medical services purchases."

"That sounds like one reasonable approach. You mentioned there are others."

"The next contributor to the high cost of medicine is the legal system. Our current legal system rewards lawyers and plaintiffs for filing frivolous lawsuits. In too many cases these frivolous filings result in underserved settlements just to reduce the potential liability and/or litigation costs. The plaintiffs and their lawyers have nothing to lose and everything to gain. If you could go to Las Vegas and keep all your winnings and have no risk of loss, what would keep you from gambling all the time? As it relates to healthcare – not only do the costs of litigation and unmerited awards increase the costs of healthcare, but the limitless, unnecessary tests requested by physicians to help avoid potential lawsuits magnifies this problem both in scope and actual costs."

"And how do you fix that?"

"The solution is to change the system to make it easier for defendants to sue plaintiffs and their lawyers when they file what is determined to be meritless lawsuits. There are already some laws which allow for this kind of recovery, but they are way too weak and require much too much support to prevail. These laws should be changed to put defendants on equal footing with plaintiffs."

"Do you see other causes for higher healthcare costs?"

"Yes, the third contributor is the fact that we spend over eighty percent of our medical expenses during the last year of life. New expensive technologies, procedures, and medications are available to help extend life, but they come at an incredible cost. Because life is so precious, many will pay anything to keep their loved ones alive, especially if they pay with someone else's money.

"The solution for this problem is not clear or without controversy given the emotional aspect of the issue. The question we need to consider is to what is everyone entitled? Are they entitled to Cadillac healthcare or Chevy healthcare? Can we as a society afford to pay over eighty percent of our healthcare costs for just one year of life? Can we afford not to? My personal opinion is that everyone is not entitled to Cadillac healthcare anymore than they are entitled to free Cadillacs.

If an individual wants to ensure that kind of coverage for them or their family members, they should either save up enough money or buy some kind of insurance coverage to make sure they get it. They should not merely be entitled to it at the expense of others, our economy, or by placing a mountain of debt on our children and grandchildren.

My key point is I should not be put in the position of making the moral decision of whether or not we pay hundreds of thousands of dollars to keep people alive for one more year. That decision should be placed in the hands of each individual who makes that choice for themselves based on the decisions they make during their life. And nobody else should be forced to make that moral decision on my behalf."

"These ideas seem to make sense, so what keeps them from being implemented?"

"It's simple, special interest groups have considerable power over elected officials who would have to pass these kinds of proposals. For instance, medical providers, especially those who provide end of life healthcare, don't want to have their incomes diminished by reducing services or making their charges more transparent. Trial lawyers will oppose legislation which discourages the filing of lawsuits, many of which are frivolous. Pharmaceutical companies and insurance companies have their own agendas. And, of course, healthcare legislation is also used by some as a redistribution of wealth system."

"How do they do that?"

"Take Medicare for instance. The original program was designed and sold to taxpayers as a pre-funded retirement benefit. You pay into a fund now a percentage of your income, up to a certain amount, and then you get it paid back in the form of free healthcare when you retire. Well, now they are talking about eliminating the cap on how much you pay each year and then charging a supplemental monthly fee to recipients who make a certain amount of income when they retire. So, by doing that, the people who pay in the most, will receive the least amount of benefit. In other words, another form of wealth redistribution."

"Well, shouldn't the people who have the most be required to contribute the most?"

"That certainly is an argument that many on the left make. Others would respond that people who make the right decisions in life, save their money and sacrifice during their working years so they can enjoy a nice retirement, shouldn't have to pay more for their healthcare because of those good decisions, while others who maybe spent more money on vacations, fancy cars, or dining out more often before they retired reap the benefits paid for by those that didn't. As I said earlier, each individual should be responsible for making that decision for themselves."

"I guess that will be a discussion for another time. Thank you, Senator Haskley, for joining us today, and we look forward to having you back soon."

"Thank you."

At the same time as this interview, Bernie Sanders, the independent and self-described Democratic Socialist from Vermont, was promoting a universal health insurance plan in which the government would control and pay for healthcare for everyone on a competing network.

Stacy Ogden, who after being the lead reporter on the lab explosions ended up being the lead reporter for the *Times* on health-related issues, had interviewed a low-profile congressman from Idaho who had a novel idea that was sure to be disregarded by both the left and the right. Congressman Daniels suggested that the government give out healthcare vouchers to everyone. They would then use those vouchers to buy private health insurance of their choosing.

His argument was that everyone in this country currently receives healthcare in one way or the other. Either they have insurance at work, or they buy personal insurance or they just don't pay because they have no money. But in the end we all pay for that healthcare. We pay for it in higher prices for goods and services to cover employers' cost of healthcare, or we pay for the insurance premiums ourselves or we pay higher prices at the emergency room to cover the cost of those who couldn't pay anything at all.

The problem is that there is no incentive to keep the cost of healthcare down. He suggested that insurance companies offer policies that provide policyholders incentives to do just that. The policies would provide cash rebates to policyholders who spent less on healthcare. In effect, part of the healthcare voucher could be turned into a cash bonus that could be used for anything. With this kind of incentive, people may choose healthier lifestyles or at least make sure they purchased the most cost-effective healthcare, realizing any savings would go in their own pocket.

During the interview, Stacy brought up Senator Haskley's concerns about the huge cost of healthcare in the last year of life. The congressman was quick to answer that his plan would also address that issue. People could choose what type of policy to purchase with their voucher. They could purchase a policy with a low deductible, but had a reasonable lifetime maximum benefit which would be large enough to provide most required benefits for one's life. However, they could choose a higher deductible plan with no maximum benefit. This type of policy would provide unlimited benefits at the later stages of life. In this way, individuals would choose what kind of later life benefits they would be entitled to rather than the government choosing or ultimately rationing that care. People could choose to sacrifice a little today by having a higher deductible, but have benefits available later if needed. Of course, some could choose to use their own money to supplement the voucher and get both.

As expected, those on the left derided the idea that wealthy people could buy a better policy and that private businesses would still basically be running the healthcare industry. And those on the right were not in favor of having the government pay for everyone's healthcare.

Interviews like this emanated from congressmen and women from both sides of the aisle for months on end. No one expected the process to go smoothly. The biggest hurdle to passing this health care legislation would occur in the Senate, but the house played an important role in making sure it ultimately passed.

Given the united Republican opposition to Democratic health care legislation in the Senate, the majority leader of the Senate would have to make sure any proposal could count on the votes of all fifty-eight Democrats and the two independent senators who caucused with them. This, in and of itself, would be difficult, considering there were disagreements on such complicated matters as the public option, employer mandates, taxing high-priced plans, and the need to keep the legislation's price tag below the President's $900 billion limit.

Milton was able to create a name for himself in this particular effort. Because of his close relationship with the pharmaceutical industry, he was able to arrange a deal between the pharmaceutical industry and Senator Baucus for an $80 billion commitment to make drugs more affordable for older Americans and thus reduce the price tag of health care reform. Of course, the deal did not come without strings—the drug companies were promised that health care reform would not involve government-negotiated prices of drugs or the importation of drugs from Canada. In a similar deal, the White House also negotiated with hospital associations for $155 billion in savings. The full terms of neither of these deals nor any record of them was ever made public.

Democrats were eager to pass a bill as soon as possible, preferably by the President's State of the Union address on January 20, 2010, but by early February at the latest. To accomplish this, Democratic congressional leaders and White House officials met in private to draft a proposal that could pass both houses. Milton, because of his chairmanship, was in attendance.

However, on January 19, 2010, Massachusetts voters elected Republican Scott Brown in a special election to fill the seat formerly held by the late Democratic Senator Ted Kennedy, subtracting one crucial vote from what had been the Democrats' sixty-vote, filibuster-proof majority. Since the Democrats had no hope of winning any Republican support for their health care proposal, Brown's election cast a pall on the health care bill's prospects for passage. A conference committee, which had been unlikely before, was now impossible.

This left the Democrats only one option to pass the legislation--the use of the Reconciliation rules.

Under these rules, legislation dealing with budget-related issues could be passed in the Senate with only a simple majority and debate and amendments were strictly limited. The only catch was that both the house and Senate must pass the exact same bill.

Thus started a series of negotiations among both liberal and moderate Democratic senators. The satisfaction of the moderates was key, as they had not been completely happy with the bill that had been reported previously to the floor.

The final reconciliation legislation was borne from negotiations between White House officials and Democratic congressional leaders, again working outside of the traditional legislative process. Though Democrats would rely on their majorities for success, differences between party factions, especially the anti-abortion and fiscal conservative blocs, influenced what they would be able to accomplish. President Obama helped initiate discussions in February 2010 with his proposal of what reconciliation should look like.

After much internal debate and many procedural hurdles, the Affordable Care Act was passed on March 25, 2010. Milton's contribution to the passage was well documented and appreciated by his peers.

CHAPTER 22

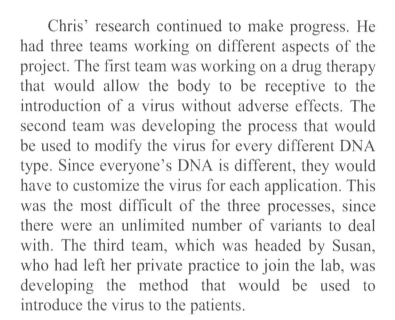

Chris' research continued to make progress. He had three teams working on different aspects of the project. The first team was working on a drug therapy that would allow the body to be receptive to the introduction of a virus without adverse effects. The second team was developing the process that would be used to modify the virus for every different DNA type. Since everyone's DNA is different, they would have to customize the virus for each application. This was the most difficult of the three processes, since there were an unlimited number of variants to deal with. The third team, which was headed by Susan, who had left her private practice to join the lab, was developing the method that would be used to introduce the virus to the patients.

It had been six years since Chris had sold his previous research to Trident. The company had dwindling cash resources and Chris had rejected the idea of submitting applications for government grants. He wanted to maintain control of the research at all costs, despite pressure from his investors.

At their latest board meeting, he had informed them that they were now ready to begin testing the therapy on animals. They would begin on rats and then move on to monkeys.

"How long will this process take?" an investor asked.

"We don't know for sure, but we expect it to be completed in less than a year. With positive results we can then begin Phase 1 trials for the FDA."

"Do we have enough cash to support this research until we finalize the therapy?" another asked.

"It will be tight, but I think we do," Chris responded.

"You realize that if we run out of money we will have to raise more capital and you could lose control of the company."

"I understand. We are progressing as fast as humanly possible."

The animal tests went very well. The drug therapy worked exactly as expected and allowed the introduction of the virus without adverse effects. The virus customization, which they thought would be the biggest hurdle, ended up being solved by Chris based on an idea he got in the middle of the night. He rushed to the lab, still wearing his pajamas, to run the calculations and write down his thoughts before he forgot them. Within a week they had perfected the process.

Figuring out how to introduce the virus to the DNA ended up being the biggest challenge. Chris and Susan worked for months on that aspect of the therapy. They tried multiple methods without success. Finally, just before Christmas of 2018, they discovered a methodology that worked. They first tried it on rats and then the monkeys. In both cases the full therapy produced the exact results they were looking for.

The modified viruses were introduced into genetic cells to compensate for abnormal genes and produced a beneficial protein. When a mutated gene caused by a disease became faulty or missing, the modified virus restored the function of the protein. The viruses introduced to the DNA remained dormant until a disease was apparent in the animal and then it automatically activated to attack the abnormal gene and replace it with a healthy one.

Further testing showed that this therapy would not only alleviate most known diseases, but actually extend the life expectancy by about forty percent. This was the holy grail that had been working so hard to achieve. But making monkeys live longer was not the goal. They would have to do human trials and go through the FDA approval process, which was no easy ordeal.

The Center for Drug Evaluation and Research "CDER," the division of the FDA responsible for drug evaluation, does not actually test drugs, although the Center's Office of Testing and Research does conduct limited research in the areas of drug quality, safety, and effectiveness.

DER is the largest of FDA's six centers and has responsibility for both prescription and nonprescription drugs. It is the responsibility of the company seeking to market a drug to test it and submit evidence that it is safe and effective. A team of CDER physicians, statisticians, chemists, pharmacologists, and other scientists reviews the sponsor's application containing the data and proposed labeling.

Chris called to set up an initial meeting with the CDER staff to discuss the steps they would have to take in order to get approval for this new therapy. He arranged a flight to Reagan National since the FDA was located in Silver Springs, Maryland, right outside the capital. Since he was going to be in DC anyway, he decided to give Milton a call to see if they could meet while he was there.

"Hey stranger, how have you been?" Milton asked.

"Very busy, as I'm sure you can imagine," Chris responded. "I don't get a chance to watch the news very much, but I have seen that you are definitely moving up the political ladder."

"You never know what to believe on television these days, but I have made some important inroads here."

"I was calling because we have finally developed the new therapy I have been working on for the last ten years, and I am meeting with the CDER next week. I thought maybe we could get together for dinner while I'm in town and we could catch up."

"That sounds great. Exactly when will you be here?"

"I arrive next Wednesday at about 6 p.m. By the time I get to the hotel it will be about seven. Maybe we can catch a late dinner."

"I happen to be free next Wednesday night. That would be perfect. Where are you staying?"

"I'm staying at the Sheraton in Silver Springs."

"Okay, I'll have a car pick you up at 7:30 and I'll make reservations for dinner."

"Thanks, look forward to seeing you."

"Me, too."

Fifteen minutes after they hung up Albert Stein received an email. "Chris Cummings research complete. Meeting with Milton Simon next Wednesday night. Details to follow."

CHAPTER 23

Milton's car picked up Chris at his hotel promptly at 7:30. They drove through the tree-lined streets of Silver Springs to a small Italian restaurant not far from the hotel. Mario's was located halfway between Chris' hotel and the FDA headquarters.

When Chris entered he immediately noticed Milton at the corner table sitting with a tall redhead. He extended his hand as he reached the table. "Hey, old friend, how're you doing?"

Milton grabbed his hand and pulled him close and gave him a big bearhug. "I'm great, how about you?" Not waiting for a reply he said, "Let me introduce you to a friend of our family, Crystal. She was at the bar when I came in and I invited her to join us."

Chris didn't believe that story. *This woman would not eat alone very often, if ever.* "Hello, Crystal, nice to meet you."

"You, too, Chris. I understand you and Milton have been friends since college."

"Yes we have, but geography and business have kept us from seeing much of each other over the years."

"That's too bad, Milton has had many nice things to say about you."

"Well, it's a shame I can't return the favor," Chris kidded.

"Some things never change," added Milton. "Sorry we started without you. Can I pour you some Chianti?"

"Of course. So I know what this guy does, how about you, Crystal, do you work?"

"Yes, I'm in public relations."

I'm sure she is, thought Chris.

"I've been in the field for over ten years," she added.

Chris and Crystal continued their friendly conversation for several minutes with a few interruptions by Milton and then the waiter taking their orders. Chris decided early on not to bring up Milton's family, thinking it may make Crystal uncomfortable.

"Okay, old boy, so tell me what you have been up to," Chris asked Milton.

"You've been in the news quite a bit."

"Like I said on the phone, you can't always believe the news."

"Don't worry, I don't. But tell me, what's it like being a popular congressman?"

"Frankly, it's a pain in the ass. First, you have to listen to all these complaints from constituents back home. Then you have to deal with your colleagues who are always wanting something from you. Then there are the archaic house rules that require you to do the weirdest things and horse trade all kinds of crap, most of which is really unimportant. Occasionally you get to work on something important like the Affordable Care Act. The rest of the time its mostly bullshit."

"But Milton, you probably get to go to a lot of great parties. I know you like that."

"You are right about that. But after a while even that loses its luster."

"So what's going to happen in the next election, Milton. Will Trump get reelected?"

"Nobody knows. The economy is riding on such a high, my friends are concerned that if something big doesn't happen between now and the election he just might. We don't even know who the Democratic nominee will be. As I'm sure you've seen there, is quite a division between the far left and the moderates in the party."

"Who will you be supporting?"

"Of course, this is confidential, but my supporters are more moderate, so I will be pulling for Joe Biden. He represents the more moderate views of the party. We have the same supporters and they expect me to support his candidacy. But don't mention that to anybody."

"Of course, what happens in Silver Springs, stays in Silver Springs," Chris joked while trying not to look at Crystal as he said it.

"I know I can count on your confidence."

"You bet."

"So how is your research going, Chris?"

"We've recently made some important breakthroughs. In fact, as I mentioned, I'm here to begin the FDA approval process for our therapy."

"What exactly is your therapy? I haven't seen anything in the press about it or in any health-related materials I read because of my position on the committee."

"We have been keeping it close to the vest. We really don't need any press, since it looks like we have enough capital to complete the project so we don't need to hype investors and there was no reason to alert potential competitors about our work."

"I understand. But now that you are going to the FDA I assume that will change."

"That's correct, but we will only provide the absolutely necessary documentation when it is required."

"You hinted the other day that this was going to be really groundbreaking."

"It is, in fact, it is probably the most important medical discovery ever."

"You say, humbly!"

"I know it sounds braggadocio, but I really believe it. We have uncovered a way to eliminate most diseases and increase life expectancies by up to forty percent."

"What? I could end up living to be over 120 years old and never get sick?"

"That's right."

"Waiter, bring us another bottle of wine," Milton shouted across the small room. "How can you possibly do that?"

"Obviously, I can't provide you or would you probably understand the scientific details, but here is the gist of it. We have created a virus that can be modified for each individual, which can then be introduced to that person's DNA cells, which when needed will attack diseases that enter the body. Normally a virus that is inserted directly into a cell does not function. But we created a carrier called a

140

vector, which has been genetically engineered to deliver the virus. The viruses are modified so they can't cause disease when used in people, but remain dormant until a cell is attacked by a disease and then it goes to work.

A sample of the patient's cells can be removed and exposed to the vector in a laboratory setting. Then we customize the virus for that individual's specific DNA and then introduce the virus back to the patient."

"You're right, I won't understand."

"Obviously, it's a lot more complicated than that."

"So what's the timeframe on getting approval for this?"

"If everything goes smoothly, which is not normally the case when you are dealing with the government, 12 to 18 months."

"Well, let me know if I can be of any help. I have contacts at the FDA."

"I'll do that."

The three of them enjoyed a nice meal while Chris and Milton reminisced about the good 'ole days. Chris tried to bring Crystal into the conversation as often as possible. By the end of the evening Crystal was wishing she was going home with Chris, not Milton.

As they finished dinner and Milton picked up the check, "I've got this. We did speak about healthcare. I can expense this."

"Are you sure?

"He's sure," Crystal added.

"And I can have my driver take you back to your hotel."

"That's not necessary. There are a couple of cabs out front at the corner and I'm only a few minutes away."

"Okay, it was great catching up. Let's not let so much time go by next time."

Chris graciously left before the other two as Milton finished paying the bill. Then Crystal and Milton got into the Lincoln Navigator and drove off toward her apartment. Milton had told Lucy he was having a late night with Chris and would just stay at a hotel out in Silver Springs since he had a meeting at the FDA the next morning anyway.

CHAPTER 24

When Milton got to his office the next morning there was an email from his father waiting for him.

"Good morning Congressman," the attractive receptionist greeted him.

"Good morning, Linda. Any messages for me?"

"Your father called and asked that you call him as soon as you were in. He tried your cell, but he said it went directly to voicemail."

"Yeah, my phone died. I'll charge it now."

When he opened his email he saw the urgent email from his father. It read – "Come home now. Urgent meeting with supporters."

He got up and closed his door and phoned home. "What's up Dad?"

"I understand you had dinner with Chris Cummings last night."

"I did. What's so important about that? And how did you know about that anyway?"

"Don't worry about how I get my information. Just book the next flight back here. We have a meeting set up for tomorrow at the house."

"I can't just leave at the spur of the moment. I have duties here."

"Son, this is not a request. I'll see you tonight," he said as he hung up.

Milton stood up, somewhat shaken by his father's tone and opened his office door. "Linda, get me a reservation on the first plane to San Francisco – first class, of course."

Because of the three-hour time change, Milton arrived in time for dinner. He and his father met in the office library for a drink before dinner. "So what's so important that I needed to fly back here at a moment's notice?"

"Chris Cummings is what's so important."

"What about Chris?"

"Did you talk about his research last night?"

"Yes."

"How much did he share with you?"

"Not too much, just that his new discovery may change the world."

"Exactly."

"Why is that a problem?"

"Our supporters, and I'm sure you know what industry they are in, have been watching his work. Imagine what impact a new therapy that kept people from getting sick would have on their industry."

"Oh, I see, but what can we do about it?"

"That's why you're here. We need to discuss our options."

"But I'm not sure that even my position on the committee can have much of an impact on that."

"That's true, but I think our friends have higher ambitions for you. We will discuss this more tomorrow. Your mother is waiting on us for dinner."

The two sojourned to the ornate dining room, where they feasted on a gourmet meal cooked by the house staff. After dinner Milton excused himself, since the jet lag and the three-hour time difference had him exhausted.

The next morning Mrs. Milton left for shopping and the staff was given the day off after preparing some refreshments for the guests who would soon arrive. At about eleven in the morning the suited gentlemen began to arrive, one at a time, in their limos. By eleven fifteen, eight men had arrived, including Albert Stein.

Theodore brought the refreshments out to the grand living room where everyone had found a seat. "Please, help yourselves," he offered.

A few of the men got up and grabbed a cup of coffee and a fresh muffin. The others declined. Albert Stein began the conversation. "Milton, I understand that you had dinner with Chris Cummings last night."

"That's correct, I did."

"Could you please recount your conversations with him?"

Milton did the best he could to repeat what Chris had told them, but the science part was a little iffy.

"Did he give you a timeframe?"

"He suggested about 12-18 months if everything went smoothly."

"I assume you realize what effect this type of development could have on our industry?"

"Of course, but I'm not sure what I can do to help."

"We will all have our responsibilities in that regard. Our first goal is to slow down the progress of the FDA approval. If we can push it out to after the election we will be in a better position to stall any ultimate approval."

"How will the election do that?" Milton asked.

"Because when our man wins the White House, you will be appointed the Secretary of Health and Human Services. In that position you will have authority over the FDA."

"I see," Milton uttered as he began to think about the consequences of that.

"In the meantime, we expect you to use your contacts at the FDA to stall the approval process."

"I understand," he agreed but was having reservations, which he did not let show, about this role and its impact on his old friend.

"You did a great job for us when Obamacare was passed. We're sure you can repeat the performance on this matter."

The meeting continued for a couple of hours as they discussed other important legislative matters. As they left, each guest offered his hand to Milton and thanked him for his service to the country. Milton wasn't so sure he was serving his country.

Albert Stein was the last to leave. "Milton, we really appreciate all your efforts on our behalf, and you can certainly count on our continued support."

"Thank you, Mr. Stein. Glad that I can be of service."

As Stein entered his limo he pulled out his cell phone and dialed. The telephone at 58 Grantham Avenue rang.

"Hello.""This is Stein, we have another job for you."

CHAPTER 25

The next morning Chris took a cab to the CDER building for his meeting with the Director. Buildings 21 and 22 were attached. The first building, with an orangish red brick with greenish windows housed the offices. Building 22 was attached by a covered walkway and housed the organization's lab.

Chris entered the main entrance and approached the reception desk. "Hello, my name is Chris Cummings. I have an appointment to meet with Director Graham."

The receptionist handed him a clipboard which had a brief questionnaire attached. "Please complete this form and I will let the Director's office know you are here."

Chris took the clipboard and found a seat in the lobby to complete it. *Typical government operation*, he thought. *Why waste an opportunity to create more paper and a job for someone to file it.*

The form was mundane. Name, address, telephone numbers, company, time of arrival, time of appointment, purpose of meeting – nothing of real import or anything they didn't already have as part of his previous submissions to set the meeting. Duplication and redundancy were two aspects of why government worked so slowly.

He returned the clipboard to the receptionist. She informed him that the Director's office had been alerted he was here and asked him to take a seat. "Someone will be down shortly to get you," she added. "Please wear this badge at all times while in the building."

About fifteen minutes later a woman, probably in her early 60s, walked over and greeted him. "You must be Dr. Cummings. I am Grace Winsten, Dr. Graham's assistant. Please follow me, he is waiting for you."

Chris followed her down the long, wide hallways for what seemed about a quarter mile. *This must be how this lady stays thin, she walks a couple of miles a day.* Finally they reached a small conference room which looked like it was attached to the Director's suite of offices. As he walked in, an overweight man, with drooping jowls and almost no hair stood to meet him. "Hello, Dr. Cummings, I am Jonathan Graham. Pleased to meet you."

"Please call me Chris. Thank you for your time."

"Please, have a seat."

As Grace was leaving she asked the men if they wanted any refreshments or something to drink."

Both declined, so she left and closed the door upon exiting.

"Well, Chris, from the application you submitted it appears you are on the brink of an extremely exciting therapy. We at the CDER look forward to working with you on its approval. I've read through the initial materials you've submitted and am excited about the opportunity to learn more. This certainly is a unique application, and as I understand it involves three separate processes. Do you intend to submit these as a combined process or as three separate therapies?"

"That's one of the reasons for my visit. I wanted to get your take on which approach would be most expeditious."

"That's a tough call. On the one hand, separate submissions would probably go faster for each, but then one of them might get bogged down and then make the whole process go even slower. Also, at the end of the separate review process, we would probably want to evaluate the entire therapeutic application anyway. I think in the end it would serve your purpose better to submit everything together."

"I understand. That's actually what I was thinking, as well."

"Everyone who starts this process expects it to move along quickly, but I want to warn you that

151

normally isn't the case. Only in instances where the therapy addresses a current health emergency do we fast track the approval process."

"Yes, I know. It's my understanding that the process could take up to eighteen months."

"That's right if everything goes smoothly. I've seen cases where it has taken years. And your therapy is very unique and consequently it could take longer."

"I hope not, but you can be assured we will respond to all your inquiries on a very timely basis to help expedite the process."

"I expected you would."

The two men continued their conversation for about another thirty minutes as Chris delved into more details about the process. "Thank you for your time, Director Graham. I look forward to working with you and your colleagues."

"You're welcome, Chris. I will have Grace escort you out. Good luck with your project," he said, leaving through the side door which apparently led to his office. A few seconds later Grace entered and led Chris back out to the receptions area. He dropped off his badge and hailed a taxi to take him back to the airport.

Back in the Director's office, Albert Stein was sitting in a comfortable leather chair which peered out of the office window. "How did your meeting go Jonathan?"

"As expected. I warned him this could be a long process." "Good, make sure it is."

CHAPTER 26

Four police cars and a fire truck rushed to Cummings Lab at two in the early morning. Apparently, a bomb exploded just outside the lab and pretty much destroyed it completely. A fire was raging while ten firemen spewed water from several directions in an ill-fated attempt to save the building.

About thirty minutes later Chris and Susan arrived. "Oh my God," Susan screamed. "What could have caused this? I don't think we had any flammable material in the lab. At least nothing that would cause this."

"You're right. I don't believe this was an accident."

"You think someone did this on purpose?"

'You remember when we were in school our lab at Stanford was blown up and then a few years later some other labs were blown up, too?"

"Yes, but those were supposedly done by pro-life extremists because of the work they were doing with fetuses."

"Supposedly is the operative word. I seem to remember this reporter from the *New York Times* was never convinced that the extremists were behind the attacks."

A policeman approached them. "You'll have to move back. This is a crime scene."

"I'm Chris Cummings and this is my wife Susan. This is... was our building."

"I'm sorry to hear that, but you'll still have to move back some. But please stay nearby. A detective will probably want to take a statement from you."

"Of course. We'll be right over there."

The blaze was finally put out after about two hours. There was truly little left of the lab. By then a couple more unmarked police cars had arrived. After speaking to one of the officers on the scene, Chris and Susan saw him point toward them. The newly arrived officer, wearing a coat and tie, approached them.

"Hello, I'm Detective Forrester. I understand that this is your building."

"It was."

"I'm sorry for your loss. Do you mind answering a few questions now, or would you rather come down to the station tomorrow?"

"Now would be fine," Chris answered.

"Okay, how long have you owned the building?"

"We initially started leasing it about twelve years ago and then we eventually bought it about nine years ago."

"What do you do in the building?"

"It's a lab. We do medical research."

"Did you house any flammable materials that could have caused this?"

"No, sir. Nothing that could do this kind of damage."

"Do you know of anyone that would want to hurt you or your business. Any enemies?"

"Not that I know of."

"What about potential competitors?"

"Not really. The kind of work we do really has no competitors."

"What kind of work is that, actually?"

"Our main focus is a new therapy that will eliminate people from getting sick and extend their life expectancy about forty percent."

"Sounds like science fiction to me. Are you really a research lab or a movie production facility?"

"I assure you we are a lab. And we have been working for fifteen years on this therapy."

"Calm down, I was just kidding."

"Maybe this isn't the best time for jokes," Susan interjected.

"Sorry, I agree. We will do our best to find out who did this."

"Do you really think that you can catch the perpetrator? There have been similar bombings at several labs in the past and they never caught the bombers."

"What labs were those?"

They spent the next thirty minutes discussing the prior bombings and Chris told him about the reporter from the *Times*. He couldn't remember her name, but was sure the detective could hunt her down.

"By the way, did you have any security cameras on the building?"

"Yes, we did, several actually."

"Is the footage stored on site or can it be retrieved remotely?"

"It's all stored in the cloud. I can access it when I get home and send you a copy if there is anything of note on it."

"Thanks, that would be helpful. Here is my card. It has my contact information and my email address to forward the video footage to."

Chris and Susan raced home to view the security camera footage. "Do you have any idea who would want to blow up our lab?" questioned Susan.

"Not really, but it may not be a coincidence that this happened soon after we made our research more public when we submitted our initial paperwork to the FDA."

"But who would want to hinder this type of discovery?"

"I don't know, but maybe the video footage will give us an indication."

They went straight to Chris' home office when they arrived and turned on his computer. He logged into the security camera program and they started watching the footage.

"I think the bomb exploded at about 1:30 am. So fast forward to midnight," Susan suggested.

Chris fast-forwarded and they started watching the video from there. For the first hour they saw nothing but a few stray cats walk by. Then at 1:05 they saw the beam of two headlights approach the building. A man, shielding his face with a Giants baseball cap, got out of the car and walked around to the back of the building. Five minutes later he returned and hurriedly left. Twenty minutes later the video stopped with a big flash.

"Well, at least we know it wasn't an accident," Susan said.

"Now all we have to do is find an average build man wearing a Giants baseball cap. Can't be more than a hundred thousand of those around here," he responded.

"Well, at least it's a lead. Send this off to Detective Forrester. Maybe they can enhance it and get something more from it."

Chris sent it off with a brief note and they decided to try and get some sleep. Susan fell asleep quickly, but Chris couldn't. He kept wondering who would do such a thing. Fortunately, they had decided long ago to back up all their research off-site. This would slow down their progress, but only for a few months until they could rebuild their lab. Fortunately, the insurance would pay for that.

CHAPTER 27

Chris and Susan immediately started looking for new lab space. They found an empty industrial space right off Highway 82 in Mountain View on Castro Street. They contacted the telephone number printed on a for rent sign attached to the building. The landlord answered and they arranged to meet that afternoon to look inside the property.

Chris was waiting fifteen minutes for the landlord before he arrived. He arrived in an old pick-up truck. A tall, lanky man, probably in his early 60s, jumped out of the truck and walked toward Chris. He wore a battered cowboy hat and old leather boots.

"I hope you weren't waiting long, I had an issue with one of our cows."

No, not long. Thanks for coming out on such short notice."

"No problem. This old place has been vacant for several months and we'll be glad to have a tenant."

"Can I ask you how a farmer from Stockton ended up owning industrial space in Silicon Valley?"

"Actually, my family owns a lot of buildings like this around here. Every time we had a bumper crop we took the extra money and bought some real estate. We've been doing that for thirty years. Probably own about twenty industrial buildings and a couple of hundred apartments," he added.

"That's fantastic. You and your family deserve everything you get for working hard and using the rewards of that effort to build on it."

"Yeah, I just hope we can keep it in the family. They keep raising taxes in California faster than we can raise rents and that puts a squeeze on us. And when my wife and I die the inheritance taxes will probably cause my kids to have to sell at least some of the properties."

"I understand. I'm dealing with the government right now myself."

"What kind of business are you planning to run out of here?" he asked.

"My company is called Cummings Lab and we do medical research."

"Oh, are you the guys who had your lab blown up a couple of days ago?"

"That's us."

"I hope that won't happen here."

"Don't worry. We are going to hire 24-hour security to watch the place. Can't afford another accident like that."

"Okay, let's take a look inside," he said as he directed Chris toward the front door.

Sam Smith showed him around the space. For the most part it was empty, but there were a few partitions up here and there. Sam said it was about 3,200 square feet in all and he wanted $6,000 a month. Chris would be responsible for utilities and any improvements he wanted to make. It wasn't going to be perfect, but Chris decided it could work. The landlord agreed to have his attorney draw up the lease papers and forward them to Chris for his review. If he were satisfied with the paperwork he could send over the company's financial statements and if everything were in order they could execute the lease.

Chris agreed and asked Sam to send him a copy of the building plans so he could get them to his architect as soon as possible.

"Don't have to wait young man, I have a copy in my truck."

They walked out together and Sam locked up. Chris picked up the plans and they bid each goodbye. From there, Chris drove straight to his architect's office to drop off the plans and then drove home to fill Susan in on his progress.

When he arrived he saw an unknown car in the driveway, a black Toyota Camry. He hustled up to the front door and walked in. He found Susan with a woman drinking tea in the dining room.

"Hi, honey. This is Stacy Ogden, from the *New York Times*. Remember her from our Stanford days?"

Stacy stood to shake his hand as he approached. "Hello, Dr. Cummings. I hope you don't mind the intrusion."

"No problem, but call me Chris. You sure work fast. I assume you're here about the bombing."

"Correct on all counts. We live in a 24-hour news cycle, so we have to act fast."

"I wish our work went so fast," he said.

"From what Susan has been telling me about your research, I wish it did, too."

"Well, I hope she didn't give away all our secrets."

"Don't worry, she used very broad brushes, but what she did explain it sounds like you are on the brink of an incredible discovery."

"We think so. Is there anything else you need from us that Susan hasn't already shared?"

"Well, I would kind of like to know your take on all these bombings. I met with Detective Forrester before coming here, and he thinks it was a professional job. The bomber used military grade C-4, just like the prior bombings. He also said the video you sent him won't be of much help since his head was completely covered and the camera didn't pick up any part of the car he drove. He must have scouted the place ahead of time to make sure he knew where all the cameras were. Do you have any thoughts on who would do this?"

"Not really. The only thing that sticks in my mind is that up till recently we have kept our research very quiet. And soon after some public information was released, we get bombed."

"Why did you release the information now?"

"We had to because we are starting the FDA approval process. Of course, we didn't make a news release, but we had to provide information to the CDER."

"What's the CDER?"

"That stands for Center for Drug Evaluation and Research. That's the division of the FDA that approves new drugs and therapies."

"And did they make a news release about your application. I didn't see one come across the wire?"

"No, they wouldn't do that, but once somebody in government knows something, everybody knows it."

"That doesn't sound like a coincidence to me."

"Me neither," added Chris.

"So what kind of a setback is this for you? I remember the other labs lost a lot of their research when they were bombed."

"That's why we backed up all our research in the cloud. Our only delay will be the time it takes to rebuild the lab. In the meantime, I told the staff to go on a well-deserved extended vacation and come back ready to turn it on."

"How long will it take to rebuild?"

"Probably a few months."

"Well, I'm going to continue to investigate these bombings. I think we have to look at who has something to gain by slowing your research."

"I guess that makes sense. Let me know if I can be of any help. And I will keep you informed if we hear anything of interest."

"Thanks, and when you're ready to really go public with your discoveries, let me know. The *Times* would love to do a feature on it."

"Will do."

After Stacy departed Susan asked, "Who would benefit by slowing our progress?"

"I think only someone who is on the same track, but I haven't heard of anybody. Of course, you don't know what you don't know."

"By the way, how did it go with the landlord?"

Chris filled her in on his meeting and dropping off the plans at the architect's office. "We should go over their as soon as we sign the lease and draw up some preliminary layouts. Now that we know the exact direction we are going, we can outfit the new lab according to those needs."

"That makes sense. So now where are you taking me to dinner?"

CHAPTER 28

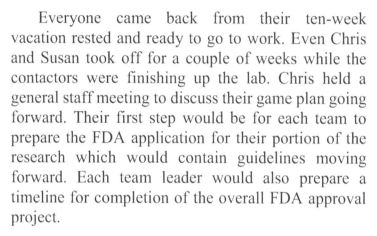

Everyone came back from their ten-week vacation rested and ready to go to work. Even Chris and Susan took off for a couple of weeks while the contactors were finishing up the lab. Chris held a general staff meeting to discuss their game plan going forward. Their first step would be for each team to prepare the FDA application for their portion of the research which would contain guidelines moving forward. Each team leader would also prepare a timeline for completion of the overall FDA approval project.

By the following week, Chris had submissions from the other two team leaders. He had been working on his during their shutdown, so it was ready first. He met with team leaders separately to go over their work and after minor adjustments to both, he boxed them up and sent them off to the appropriate contacts at CDER.

Everyone kept moving forward, but some progress would be limited until they heard back from the FDA. After a few weeks went by without any word, Chris decided to call Director Graham directly, something he preferred not to do until it was absolutely necessary.

After being put through to the Director's office, he was told he was not in the office. Chris asked his assistant to have him call back at his earliest opportunity. He was anxious for some kind of response, but had no alternative but wait to hear back.

Two more weeks went by and there was no word from anyone at the FDA. Director Graham had not even called back. Chris finally decided to have his lawyers write a formal letter to the CDER asking for a response. After all, they had just submitted preliminary proposals which outlined how the process would move forward. It shouldn't take much time to review that.

The letter must have had an impact, because within a couple of days they received their first response from CDER. They were finally on their way to complete Phase 1 trials. They had already performed many of these tasks prior to starting the work with the regulators, so it went quickly. Within a few months they made their first Phase 1 submission.

They expected a longer wait for a response this time, since the data had to be analyzed by several different groups inside the CDER. However, they expected some initial questions during the process. Once again, there was an inordinate amount of delay. Finally, after a few months they began to get some questions from one team inside the FDA.

Of course, they followed up immediately, as Chris had promised Director Graham they would. The same level of urgency did not come from the other side. It took over a year to get a final response to their Phase 1 trials.

It was already September of 2019 when they began submitting the initial Phase 2 materials. Unfortunately, the same delays raised their ugly heads again. It was at this time that Chris made a decision that would have a lasting impact on their research. He decided to move the lab to a more friendly regulatory environment. He informed the team that they would be moving the lab to the Netherlands and simultaneously work with European regulators to get approval for their therapy. He explained at the staff meeting that the company would cover all the costs of moving and that the move would be temporary until they had received the FDA approval. It will just be like a working European vacation.

Everyone was excited about the move. A few had never been to Europe before, and they relished the chance to visit a new area of the world. It took two months to pack everything up and ship it out to Amsterdam. Chris had found a perfect space about fifteen miles out from the city center in a small city called Naarden. It was a twenty-minute drive south on the A-1 highway about halfway between Amsterdam and the University of Utrecht, where they could hire some student interns. This move would not be cheap, but in the long run, the shorter timeframe would more than make up for the added cost. In addition, the European Medicines Agency (EMA) had recently moved from London to Amsterdam, so they would be able to have onsite meetings to push through their agenda.

They were in their new lab in January, right before the shit hit the fan. The Covid-19 pandemic hit the world hard two months later. This would surely have put a roadblock on FDA approval, since all their resources would be focused on that. Chris was afraid the same delays would happen at the EMA because of the pandemic. But fortunately he made a significant contact at the EMA prior to their move who promised to help push his research through.

The lab continued to submit data to both agencies. As expected, the CDER provided little, if any, response. However, the EMA was extremely helpful, even during the pandemic, partially because Chris' contact, Toby De Vries, thought the research could have an impact on the current health crisis.

By mid-2020 they were ready for Phase 3 trials in Europe. They advertised for human volunteers. Since the therapy was fairly radical, it was difficult to find volunteers. However, the hopes of not getting sick anymore and maybe being immune from the current Covid-19 virus motivated enough people to apply for the paid experiment. Given the economic state, it was probably the cash payments that was truly the motivating factor.

In order to get a true picture of the therapy's efficacy, they did a double-blind study. The results were very promising. Over eighty percent of the volunteers receiving the actual treatment were found to be immune from any disease they were exposed to, including the Covid-19 virus. The other twenty percent or so had a problem with their body accepting the modified virus vector which is introduced to their DNA. The team would continue to work on the modification process in an attempt to reach a one hundred percent efficacy.

By the end of the year, they had reached a ninety-seven percent efficacy rate with no meaningful adverse side effects. They submitted the final paperwork to the EMA and asked for an emergency use approval since it could immunize people from the Covid virus.

CHAPTER 29

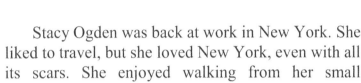

Stacy Ogden was back at work in New York. She liked to travel, but she loved New York, even with all its scars. She enjoyed walking from her small Manhattan flat to One Times Square, at 1475 Broadway, the New York Times Building, a 25-story, 363-foot-high skyscraper, designed by Cyrus L. W. Eidlitz, located at 42nd Street and Broadway.

Since she had been back from her trip west to investigate the bombings at Cummings Lab, with no meaningful discoveries, she was busy with other stories. She submitted a brief article upon her return about the bombing, but without much new to report, it found its way to page 23. When the Covid virus hit at the beginning of 2020, she had plenty of work on her plate as the Times' lead health reporter.

It was one of her hardest stories to cover since all the experts seemed to disagree or change their own opinions on a daily basis. Wear masks one day, don't wear them the next. Stay at home or patronize your local businesses. When Trump halted planes from coming from China, he was called a racist. Not long afterwards he was accused of not acting fast enough.

It became obvious that not only was this to be a major health crisis, but a political football, as well.

Before the crisis, there was little evidence with a booming economy that Trump, despite all his inappropriate character faults, would win reelection. Now the Democrats had an issue they could use to unseat him. Everything else had failed. Whether it was Russian collusion or the Ukrainian impeachment effort, he successfully deflected them all.

In the meantime, the Democrats had their own problems. They were divided between the far-left progressives, led by Bernie Sanders and the more moderate establishment Democrats led by the aging Joe Biden. In the end, they decided the country was not yet ready for such a progressive message and eventually the establishment Democrats prevailed and got everybody to fall in line behind Biden.

At the peak of the pandemic in the summer of 2020, Stacy tried to reach Chris for an update on his project, since it may have an impact on the virus. That's when she first found out he had moved his lab to the Netherlands. She found his contact information and called out to him.

"May I speak to Dr. Cummings, please," she asked the telephone receptionist.

"Who may I say is calling?"

"It's Stacy Ogden, from the *New York Times*."

"Please hold, I will see if he is available," she responded.

A few seconds later, "Hi Stacy. Haven't heard from you in a while."

"As you can imagine, I've been pretty busy. Looks like you have too."

'Yes, it's been pretty hectic, but very productive."

"Why did you move to Europe?"

"The FDA approval process was taking too long. They kept putting up meaningless roadblocks and they didn't respond to us on a timely basis. We hoped that the EMA would act more expeditiously."

"Have they?"

"Actually, they have, in spite of the other issues facing them at this time."

"Does that mean that your process can help the current crisis?"

"We just completed human trials and it does work. However, it won't be a universal answer to the problem because of the costs. The best hope for the Corona virus will be a vaccine that can be administered more quickly and cost effectively."

"And where do you think we are in that regard?"

"I've been too busy with my research to keep up completely, but from what I've read, I think by the end of the year we may have a couple of successful vaccines. It looks like there are a couple dozen companies that are making progress. I just hope the regulators don't get in their way."

"Like they did to you?"

"Yeah, I've heard a few complaints from some of the smaller companies that seem to have their progress impeded."

"Well, I guess we can only hope and pray for a quick solution."

"Probably hard work and some brain power will produce a quicker solution."

"Thanks for your time, Chris. We probably both better get back to work then."

"Of course, good hearing from you, Stacy."

Stacy rang her editor's assistant and asked to set a time to meet. They set a meeting for the next day at noon. The assistant suggested they could have lunch together. Stacy agreed and set off to do some research to prepare for the meeting. She considered herself lucky to find out that all FDA records are computerized and were open to public inspection, though she figured few people were ever interested in perusing this mundane information. But Stacy now had an agenda.

She had already been wondering if certain large pharmaceutical companies had an edge over newcomers or even some established companies when it came to getting FDA cooperation with their new therapies. After talking with Chris, her interest was piqued even further. She spent literally the whole day and into the night reviewing FDA actions and responses. The more she looked, the more evident it became that there were about eight companies that got much quicker reviews and responses from the CDER than their competitors. She even got access to a few disturbing emails, which were probably meant to be deleted, that confirmed her suspicions. She was ready for her lunch meeting.

At exactly noon Stacy walked over to her editor's office. She could see through the glass walls that he was still on the phone. He held up one finger, indicating he would be just a minute. Two minutes later he walked out to greet her. "Hey, Stacy, how are you?"

"Fine, sir. Thanks for taking time to meet with me."

"No problem, we all have to eat anyway. The only problem is finding someplace to do it these days." At that he turned to his assistant and asked if she had made a reservation for them somewhere.

"Yes I have. Reservation for two at Havana Central. They have outdoor dining. It's just a few blocks away and the reservation is for 12:30."

"Thanks, Cyndi."

Stacy and Martin Grimes took the elevator to the first floor and strode off toward 46th street. Martin was a giant of a man. At least six foot five and weighed in at about 260 pounds. He had been working at the *Times* since he graduated from college. A knee injury his senior year dashed any hopes of an NFL career. He started as a junior reporter and worked his way up to his current position.

When they arrived at the restaurant, they were guided to a nice sidewalk table for two and given menus. "My assistant knows I love Cuban food. Everything here is good. My favorite is the fried pork with black beans and rice with a side of plantains."

"So you come here often?"

"What's it look like," he responded while tapping his protruding stomach.

Stacy ignored his rhetorical question and delved into the menu. A few moments later the waiter arrived to take their order. Martin ordered the pork and Stacy ordered ropa vieja. "Do you know that is the national dish of Cuba?" Martin asked her.

"No I didn't. It just sounded good. I'm not sure I have ever eaten Cuban food."

"You're going to love it. Okay, so why are we meeting?"

Stacy took the next twenty minutes while they were waiting for lunch to fill him in on her thoughts and research. She told him about her concerns about the FDA approval process and that the records she had researched so far indicated a significant preference toward certain companies. She hadn't had time yet to cross reference those preferences with potential political conflicts, but had an inkling that she would ultimately find some. She also indicated that the bombings she had previously reported on may be connected, as well.

"How would those bombings be connected?" he asked.

"Well, think about it. Most of these labs, as far as I could uncover, were researching ways to alleviate sicknesses. Especially, the last one at Cummings Lab. Chris Cummings, who I have been speaking with for many years now, has just finished Phase 3 trials in Europe for a therapy that will keep people from getting almost any disease and extend life expectancy up to forty percent. And guess whose research was stymied by the FDA and literally forced him to move his lab to Europe? And who will lose out if that therapy gets commercialized?"

178

"Drug companies?"

"You got it."

"So what do you need from me?"

"I want your blessing to go after this. You know going after big pharma is a big risk and so is going after some elected officials who may be connected, as well. To do this right will take a lot of time and I would have to focus entirely on this even though the current crisis is an important story right now."

"If what you surmise is true, this could be even bigger. I'll get someone else to over the Covid issues. And don't worry about ruffling feathers. That's our job."

"Thanks, boss. I figured that was what you would say."

"I'm that predictable?"

"No, you're that committed to doing what's right. I wish I could say that about everyone in journalism today."

Martin wasn't sure the last remark applied to him.

CHAPTER 30

The celebration started as soon as the official word arrived. The EMA approved the therapy for emergency use in Europe. Even the investors from the U.S. flew in to join in the festivities. Since it was for business, they got a Covid pass. Susan had ordered a fully catered affair and Chris went to the local liquor store to pick up the champagne and various other bottles of celebratory alcohol. The party went on for hours as everyone needed a release after their hard work for the last few years.

The next morning, though, it was back to business. They now had to plan the therapy's commercialization. That included coming up with a name for it and considering some legal issues. Chris and his investors scheduled a meeting for 10 a.m. to begin those discussions.

The most important question facing them was how to protect their intellectual property. As they had previously discussed, the patent approach was risky since bigger players could make minor modifications and basically steal the work. They decided to invite the European branch of their U.S. law firm to join the conversation by Zoom.

They were able to arrange a call within the hour. Neal Holliday and George Leishman from the London office joined via Zoom. After some congratulatory comments they began to consider the issues at hand.

"Here's our dilemma," started Chris. "Your U.S. partners told us that if we patent the process, a bigger company may very well make minor modifications to our work and get away with it. If we don't patent it, then we must fully control its commercialization, which would vastly limit our ability to provide it to large numbers and the cost would go up dramatically. And if we license it to others, the research might be leaked and we end up with less protection than if we patented it."

"Unfortunately, you are correct," responded Neal. "If you patent the process it is more than likely that a larger, more capitalized company will attempt to steal it. The minor modifications they make would probably not stand up to a court fight, but that litigation could last years and you may not be able to afford it."

"The only people that ever make out in that type of fight are the lawyers," commented one of the investors.

"Unfortunately, that is correct, also," George Leishman added.

"So what should we do?" questioned Chris.

"If you want to completely avoid your research being compromised, you will have to totally control its commercialization," Holliday responded.

"That means we have one clinic and we can only perform about ten operations a day. We will have to cost out what charge will be necessary to recoup our investment and provide a reasonable return to all our stakeholders," Chris suggested.

"That's probably right until better patent protection laws are passed and even with those, larger companies may very well still opt to accept protracted litigation. It will still be cheaper than the alternative development costs."

The group discussed some other issues and potential ideas for another hour or so before ending the Zoom call. Chris suggested that they adjourn the meeting and allow him to meet with his CFO to formulate a plan and come up with some numbers. They decided to meet again the following afternoon. The staff was meeting after lunch to discuss a name for the therapy anyway.

After lunch Chris, Susan, and four other staff members congregated in the conference room to toss some name ideas around. It wasn't an easy task. They didn't want to use the word virus anywhere in the name, especially based on what was happening right now. They also didn't want to use a term that sounded too medical or complicated, even though it was both.

After about an hour Susan suggested they just call it "The Procedure." Everyone quickly agreed. It was simple and didn't sound too scary.

Chris thanked everyone for their participation and went off to meet with his CFO.

"Okay, Melissa, we have to crunch some numbers," Chris started. "We have decided that in order to protect our research, we are going to have to completely control its commercialization. In other words, we will have just one clinic and perform only ten operations a day. At least for now. So we need to determine what we will have to charge to make the numbers work."

"I can do that, but will need some additional data. First, I will need the raw cost of the products used in the operation."

"By the way," Chris interrupted. "We have decided to call it 'The Procedure'."

"Okay, I'll need the raw cost of the product used in The Procedure. I'll need to know who will be performing each of the three processes, where you intend to perform them, how much time each process will take, whether or not you will need a recovery room and how it will be staffed. With that information, I can start crunching the numbers and then we can review my preliminary thoughts and fine tune them."

"I'll get that stuff to you over the next few days," Chris answered as he left her office and walked down to Susan's office.

"I was just meeting with Melissa and we need to put together some data for her so she can come up with some financial analysis for us."

"No problem. Want to start over dinner? I made us reservations at Tutto Fresca."

"Sounds good."

They left the building and drove to their favorite Italian restaurant. They never noticed the brown sedan following them.

CHAPTER 31

Stacy started by cataloging all the information she had so far. She had scoured through the FDA files and used a spreadsheet to analyze which firms received the quickest responses. According to her work so far, there were eight pharmaceutical companies that appeared to receive preferential treatment. There was actually a wide disparity between those eight firms and all the others.

Her next step was to see if there were any political connections between those particular companies and any elected officials who may have influence over the FDA. She figured her starting point would be to look at political contributions. Unfortunately, most large contributions don't go directly to candidates, but are made through political action committees that spend money on behalf of candidates. So she had to also research records of the PACs that were supported by these firms.

It didn't take long to see that these firms and their employees were substantial donors to many elected officials on both sides of the political theater. A major portion of the contributions were, as expected, made to congressional members who sat on committees related to health care. But through her further research she found that there was a particular PAC called Healthcare for America that was funded exclusively by these eight firms. And that funding was in seven figures from each company.

Stacy ordered the federal election commission records to see what activity the Healthcare for America PAC was involved with. When she received the records, they showed that the PAC had spent hundreds of thousands to elect three particular candidates – Herbert Stonewall, a Republican from Tennessee who was the ranking member of the House Ways and Means Committee, John Knight, a Democrat from New York who was on the health subcommittee, and Simon Milton.

She decided to take all this information to her editor and discuss the next steps. They met the following day in his office. "So tell me what you've got?" he asked.

"No smoking gun, yet, but a lot of circumstantial evidence that something is definitely not kosher. I've found that eight pharmaceutical companies get special treatment from the FDA compared to most others and that those same eight firms have created and support a political action committee called Healthcare for America. I also found out that PAC provided substantial support to three specific candidates – one Republican and two Democrats."

"Sounds like a good beginning. What's your next step?"

"Here's where it is going to get interesting. I'll have to start interviewing the company executives, employees at the FDA, and these three congresspersons. That is sure to start ruffling some feathers. Do you have any suggestions about the order of those interviews?"

"I'd probably start with the FDA. You can use the current Covid crisis as an excuse for the interview and then interject some questions about this preferential treatment. Based on what you find out there, we can decide who should be next."

"That sounds like a good plan. I'll try to set up an appointment at the FDA right away and let you know the results."

Upon returning to her office she telephoned the FDA and asked to be connected with the current FDA Director. Thomas Dryer came on the line and asked, "This is Director Dryer, may I help you?"

"Hello, Director Dryer. My name is Stacy Ogden, a reporter from the *New York Times*. I am researching a story on the approval process for the Covid vaccines and wondered if we could meet to discuss it?"

"I'd be happy to meet, but you would get better information if you met with our Director of the CDER.

They are mostly responsible for approving new drugs."

"That makes sense. Who might that be?"

"His name is Jonathan Graham. Let me give you his contact information."

After receiving the information, she thanked him and hung up. She redialed the new number and asked to speak with Director Graham. After a few minutes delay Dr. Graham's assistant finally answered the phone. "May I help you?"

"Hello, my name is Stacy Odgen, with the *New York Times*. Director Dryer suggested I call Director Graham to provide me some information for an article I am writing about the Covid vaccine approval process. Is he available?"

"Let me check with him." After a few more minutes she came back on the line and told her she would put her through.

"Hello, this is Jonathan Graham. I understand that you are wanting some information on the Covid-19 vaccine approval process."

"Yes, I am doing an in-depth article about it for the *Times* and wondered if could meet to discuss it?"

"As you can imagine it is terribly busy around here, but maybe I can find a little time to meet and share some information with you. The public certainly has a right to know how their tax dollars are working for them."

"My schedule is probably more open than yours. What would work best for you?"

"Let me take a quick look at my calendar. It looks like next Tuesday morning at 10 a.m. would work."

"That will work for me also."

"Please give me your number in case something comes up and I have to reschedule."

Stacy gave him her contact information and thanked him for his time. "I look forward to our meeting," she added. *You probably won't.*

Not wanting to be late and having never been to that area before, she arrived thirty minutes early. She cooled her heels in the parking lot and entered the lobby at 9:55. She checked in at the front desk, got her badge and waited to be brought to the Director's office. At exactly 10, Grace Winsten arrived to escort her back.

Graham stood as she entered and offered her a fist pump. "A new world we live in," he said.

"Yes, it is," she replied.

"So, what can I tell you?"

"Let's start at the beginning. How many companies have submitted applications for Covid vaccine approvals?" she asked as she turned on her recorder.

"I don't have the exact number in my head, but I would say roughly ten."

"Are all of these coming from major companies, or are their smaller firms that believe they can develop a vaccine as well?"

"I think there is a mix."

"Can you briefly describe, in layman's terms, the approval process?"

"Sure. I'll try. First, the sponsor submits an Investigational New Drug application to us, IND for short, based on the results from initial testing that includes the drug's composition and manufacturing, and develops a plan for testing the drug on humans. Of course, we require the sponsor to test new drugs on animals first, for toxicity. Multiple species are used to gather basic information on the safety and efficacy of the compound being researched. Then we review the IND to assure that the proposed studies, generally referred to as clinical trials, do not place human subjects at unreasonable risk of harm. We also verify that there are adequate informed consent and human subject protections. There are typically a small number of healthy volunteers used in this phase.

"The goal here in this phase is to determine what the drug's most frequent side effects are, if any. In the next phase a much larger number of patients are used to determine its effectiveness. This goal is to obtain preliminary data on whether the drug works in people who have a certain disease or condition. For controlled trials, patients receiving the drug are compared with similar patients receiving a different treatment--usually a placebo, or a different drug. Safety continues to be evaluated, and any short-term side effects are studied.

"At the end of Phase 2, we and sponsors discuss how large-scale studies in Phase 3 will be done. The typical number of patients used in Phase 3 is still larger. These studies gather more information about safety and effectiveness, study different populations and different dosages, and uses the drug in combination with other drugs. If all of this proves effective, the drug sponsor formally asks us to approve a drug for marketing in the United States by submitting an NDA. An NDA includes all animal and human data and analyses of the data, as well as information about how the drug behaves in the body and how it is manufactured. After an NDA is received, we have 60 days to decide whether to file it so it can be reviewed. If we file the NDA, our Review team is assigned to evaluate the sponsor's research on the drug's safety and effectiveness and ultimately approve or reject the drug. I hope that wasn't too opaque."

"No, that was perfect. I'm sure our readers will want to know how this process works, especially at a time like this. But I am glad I'm recording this. How long does the total process take?"

"It can take up to eight to ten years in some cases."

"Wow, that's a long time. I hope it doesn't take that long to approve a Covid-19 vaccine."

"In this case we are fast tracking the process because of the current emergency. We also can permit 'emergency use' in cases like this which also speeds up the process."

"How long do you predict it will take for this vaccine?"

"You never know for sure, but based on the current information I have, we may be able to grant emergency use by the end of the year."

"That would be good. I was also wondering, since you have submissions by maybe ten different organizations how do you prioritize which ones you work on?"

"We try to be fair and work on those based on their dates of submission, but in reality our scientists have to evaluate which submissions they believe had the best shot at being successful."

"So who is responsible for making the final decision?"

"That would be me, but I make it based solely on the scientific reports I receive from our staff."

"I see. Are those reports available for public inspection?"

"I'm afraid not. They contain confidential information which we are not allowed to share."

"I understand. Before our meeting today I did a little research about previous applications and I was wondering if you could comment on it. Let me show you what I found."

Stacy pulled out the spreadsheet she had printed. It was fifteen pages long. "I was trying to evaluate the response times from the FDA as it related to submissions from different companies. Here are all the results, but we can turn to a summary here on the last page. My investigation seems to indicate that there are eight specific companies which receive responses from the CDER much more quickly than any others. Here is the list of those companies. Can you suggest a reason for that?"

Graham was silent for a moment, trying feverishly to find an appropriate answer. "Of course, I would have to review all of your data before making an official comment, but I can only imagine that it is coincidental."

"That would have to be a lot of coincidence since my data was gathered from over ten years."

"Well, I will certainly look into that, but I'm afraid our time is up for today," he said as he rose to escort her out of his office. "Grace, please help Ms. Ogden out."

"Thank you for your time Director Graham. Oh, here, please keep this spreadsheet and let me know if you have a further comment regarding it," she said as she handed him the pages.

"Of course, I will."

Stacy figured, as she was being escorted out, that this was probably the last time she would be permitted in this building. She didn't know how right she was.

As soon as Stacy left, Graham closed the doors to his office and reached inside the bottom drawer on his desk and pulled out a cell phone. He pushed one button to dial. "What do you need, Graham?" questioned the receiver of the call.

"I think we have a problem. A reporter from the *Times* just interviewed me and basically implied that we have been favoring certain companies. She had a lot of research to support her implication."

"How did you handle it?"

"I just told her that wasn't the case and I would look into it."

"What was the reporter's name?"

"Stacy Odgen."

"Okay, we'll handle it. Don't have any further contact with her."

"Understood."

CHAPTER 32

Chris gave Melissa all the data she should need to put together some projections. With only an extremely limited number of operations being able to be performed each day, the cost was going to be much higher than Chris expected - $48,000 per operation. Everyone agreed that it was too much, but without other protection alternatives they would have no choice. The benefits were obviously worth it, but they were hoping to make it more affordable.

Back home in the U.S., Biden had just been elected and the bitter political divide was increasing despite the new president's verbal call for unity. The signing of over 40 executive orders undoing conservative actions during the last four years didn't help. Concerns over the election results also polarized the country and even ignited a surge against the Capitol by about two hundred extemists which the left used to demonize all Trump voters.

Social media also became a spotlight as companies began making unilateral decisions about who to censor. It started by merely canceling Trump's Twitter feed, but then began to expand to cover many Americans espousing views contrary to the current administration's. Within weeks, a popular conservative social platform was completely taken down. The ruling class had now found a way to silence its opponents and it used it in various ways.

Stacy Ogden, while continuing to investigate the potential FDA scandal, saw that YouTube had taken down a video of a doctor's testimony before Congress' Committee on Homeland Security and Governmental Affairs in which he cited the use of a widely available drug called ivermectin, as a potential early treatment and prevention of Covid-19. The drug, which is widely available to treat tropical diseases caused by parasites, showed promising results from a study done in Argentina. In the study, eight hundred healthcare workers received ivermectin, while another 400 did not. Of the eight hundred, not a single person contracted Covid-19, while more than half of the four hundred did.

She noticed that Senator Ron Miller had complained about the video censorship and requested an interview with him. His office was a little skeptical about a *New York Times* reporter writing anything favorable about a conservative's position, given their recent editorial history, but accepted the invitation to meet.

The meeting was scheduled the next day in the Senator's office. After exchanging pleasantries, the meeting began with the senator criticizing U.S. health agencies, claiming that they have failed to put money and research into exploring "repurposed, cheap, generic drugs," like the one in Dr. Kory's findings.

"I'm actually investigating some potential improper activities within some U.S. health agencies right now. That's one of the reasons I wanted to meet. I wonder if you could comment on YouTube's decision to remove Dr. Kory's testimony."

I would be glad to. Since we had that hearing on December 8, the views of that video rose to over eight million. Then out of nowhere I got notified January 27 that it wasn't passing the YouTube censors, so they were going to take it down off of our website and they also took it off of Fox News Now's. This is dangerous when you have censorship of information. You know, Louis Brandeis, the Supreme Court justice had a decision almost one hundred years ago in 1927 that actually dealt with falsehoods and fallacies that might cause societal harm and he said, 'the remedy to be applied is more speech, not enforced silence.' That was wise back then, but we're moving in the exact opposite direction now. We have had two hearings on early treatment. The lead witness in my first hearing has been fired by his institution because he testified, basically. Dr. Kory is being ostracized and vilified. This makes no sense whatsoever. Our health agencies have failed us by not spending money, time and effort exploring repurposed, cheap, generic drugs."

"Why do you think they are being censored or worse?"

"Could it be because Remdesivir for example is $3,200 for a treatment and these drugs are about $20 for a treatment? Maybe it's that economic incentive, but it's a travesty regardless, and the fact that you have these frontline doctors that are risking their lives, having the courage and compassion to treat patients versus the NIH guidelines which basically say go home, isolate yourself, be afraid, do nothing until you get sick enough and then we'll try and save your life in the hospital."

"What do you think we can do about it?"

"First, we have to stop censoring contrary views. Before I was elected to Congress, I ran my own business. I always encouraged my managers to express their opinions, especially if they disagreed with me. I told them that if we both agreed on everything, one of us is not necessary. They took that to heart and it is one of the reasons our company was successful. Second, we must make sure that Crony Capitalism is eradicated from our system. We can't have people in power using their influence to help certain businesses as the expense of others and the whole population. And third, we have to stop the political bickering. Our constituents expect us to find and implement solutions to their problems, not spend our time throwing meaningless accusations at each other."

"I for one, think you have some great insight into the problems facing our country," said Stacy.

"You may be the only reporter at the Times that feels that way."

"I hope not, but I will be sure to use some of this information in my article."

"I look forward to reading it."

"Thank you for your time, Senator."

"You're welcome," he responded as he escorted her to the door.

When Stacy got back to her office she noticed some news about Cummings Lab come across the wire. They had just set up a clinic in Amsterdam to start offering The Procedure to patients. The cost of $48,000 for each operation came as a surprise to her. She used the contact information in the story to call Chris. Because of the time difference, it was already late in the Netherlands, so she got voicemail. She left a message for Chris and hoped he would call her back the next day.

In the meantime, she got back to her current investigation. She started by writing up some notes about her interview with Senator Miller. She then made a list of some of the drug companies that received slower responses from the CDER. She thought getting some input from them before she met with the firms receiving preferential treatment might clarify the process. She started making calls and set up three Zoom meetings for the following week. She called it a day and walked home to enjoy a quiet evening with a nice bottle of Cabernet.

On her walk home, she thought she noticed someone following her. It was a man wearing a Giants baseball cap that made him stick out. In New York you could be shot or worse wearing that hat. She began to quicken her pace and either he realized he had been discovered or he wasn't following her since she didn't see him anymore after she turned right at the next corner.

I must be getting paranoid she thought as she continued her walk home.

Early the next morning her cell phone rang as she was getting dressed. Since it was a foreign number she assumed it was Chris returning her call. "Hello?"

"Hi Stacy, this is Chris."

"Thanks for returning my call and congratulations."

"Thanks, it has been a long hard road, but we finally made it."

"I see you've opened a clinic in Amsterdam to perform the operations. Is that because you still don't have the FDA approval?"

"That's it. We're probably at least a year away from approval in the U.S. Everyone has enjoyed some time in Europe, but I think they are also ready to go home. We can do that once the FDA approves us."

"Can you pinpoint why the FDA process has taken so much longer than in Europe?"

"Nothing in particular, they just respond so slowly to our submissions. I guess they're busy with the Covid stuff."

"Maybe, but I have been investigating some unusual activity surrounding this process at CDER and there may be a more sinister reason."

"What might that be?"

"I'm not ready to say quite yet. I need all the facts before I make a specific allegation."

"I understand. It would be nice if all journalists took that position."

"So tell me about The Procedure."

"It's a three-part process. First, we give the patient a new drug we developed, which makes their system acceptable to our treatment. Then we take a sample of their DNA and run it through our testing equipment, which analyzes it and then produces a customized

202

vector virus which will be introduced into their genes in a very specific way. Once the virus is ready, my wife and I introduce it during a thirty-minute procedure. The patient has to stay in a recovery room for about two hours and then they can go home."

"That's it?"

"Yes."

'And it works?"

"Yes, Stacy it works. No one who has received The Procedure has gotten sick, and in follow-up tests we can see that the aging process slows by about forty percent. In other words, if you receive the treatment when you are twenty, and we won't offer it before that age, by the time you are sixty, you will look and feel like you are forty-six. By the time you reach a hundred, you will look and feel like sixty-eight."

"Wow, that's incredible. I wish I had an extra forty-eight grand sitting around. I guess I'm going to get old like most people."

"I know, The Procedure is more expensive than we wanted, but our attorneys told us that the only way to protect our research was to completely control its commercialization. Performing only ten operations a day is what causes us to charge so much."

"I understand. If I had spent most of my life creating something so wonderful, I would want to protect it as well."

"Not only spending most of my life, but almost all my money, too. Fortunately, even at ten a day, we should be able to recoup my and my investors' investment and make an appropriate profit for the time and risk we took to develop it."

"Good for you. I appreciate the call back. Let's keep in touch. In the meantime, I'm going to write an article for the paper about your Procedure. Maybe that will give the FDA a kick in the pants so you can come home sooner."

"Thanks, Stacy. Unfortunately, I don't think the FDA responds to a kick in the pants, but it can't hurt."

"At least I can try," she replied. *By the time I'm done, it will be more than a kick in the pants.*

"Good luck, then and we'll keep in touch," Chris said as he hung up.

CHAPTER 33

Following his election, Biden began the process of identifying nominees for his Cabinet. Before any nominations are made, the White House Office of Presidential Personnel vets a list of candidates, including suggestions provided by members of Congress and special interest groups. A chosen nominee then must pass through a series of investigations by the Federal Bureau of Investigation, Internal Revenue Service, the Office of Government Ethics and an ethics official from the agency to which the position is assigned. The nominee must also fill out the Public Financial Disclosure Report and questionnaires related to his or her background check.

The process begins when the president provides a written nomination to the Senate, where it is read on the floor and assigned a number. This starts the Senate's procedure of Advice and Consent.

The nomination is passed to the Senate committee with jurisdiction over the appointed position. Committee hearings allow a close examination of the nominee, looking for partisanship and views on public policy. They can also summon supporters and opponents to testify. Committees are permitted to conduct their own investigations into the nominees, as they are not always provided with the information gathered by the White House's investigation. Once committee hearings are closed, most committees have a set amount of time before a vote is taken on whether the nominee is reported to the Senate favorably, unfavorably or without recommendation. They also have the option not to act on the nominee. If action is taken, the committee notifies the executive clerk. The nomination is then given a number and added to the Executive Calendar of the Senate.

The new president was considering several potential nominees for Secretary of Health and Human Services (HHS), but was persuaded by some of his most ardent supporters to pick Milton Simon. They used his efforts to pass the Obamacare legislation as the main argument for his nomination.

February 2 was Milton's turn to face the hot seat in front of the Senate Committee on Health, Education, Labor and Pensions. He wanted to bring counsel with him, but he was told it would create bad optics, so he went alone. He arrived at exactly 10 a.m. and was escorted to the desk facing the Senators.

Since the Senate was split 50/50 between Republicans and Democrats, each party had eleven members on the committee. The Chairman called the meeting to order and began by welcoming Mr. Simon to the proceedings. He gave a brief introduction of Milton where he pointed out his qualifications for office which relied heavily on his education and service in Congress, since he had little other background which qualified him for this job.

He then asked Milton to rise and swore him in. For the next five minutes he asked him several questions for which Milton had canned answers. It was typical for the party in power to provide an easy cadre of questions to provide rest between what was sure to be more hostile treatment from the opposing party members.

After his questioning he recognized the Senator from Tennessee to proceed with his questions.

"Thank you, Chairman Green. Welcome to the Committee, Mr. Simon. We look forward to hearing a little more color on your background. To begin with, I understand that you began your career, right out of law school, at Madison Walsh?"

"That's correct, Senator."

"Is it true that Madison Walsh had several large pharmaceutical companies as clients?"

"It was a long time ago, but yes, I believe that is true."

"I'm surprised you don't remember it more clearly since I understand that you actually worked directly on several of their issues."

"I had several responsibilities at the firm and I do remember spending time on some issues that related to these firms," Milton responded as sweat began forming on his forehead.

"Do you believe that based on your previous involvement with big pharma that you can act in the best interest of Americans rather than your previous clients?" the Senator continued.

"Of course, I am committed to serving the country in the best way possible and all of its citizens."

"Glad to hear that. Speaking of serving your country, I think everyone here is aware that you were influential in getting the Affordable Care Act passed ten years ago."

"I'm not sure you could say that I was influential, but I did contribute to its passage," Simon interjected.

"As I recall it was you who worked out a deal with the pharmaceutical industry to support the legislation."

"You're correct. I did persuade the industry to contribute eighty billion dollars toward the program to make sure its final cost was below the limits your party imposed on its passage."

"In return for that eighty billion I understand that the industry received two important benefits. First, they would not have regulatory oversight, and drugs from Canada or Mexico would not be permitted to be imported. That provided drug companies about three trillion dollars in benefits in return for their eighty-billion-dollar contribution. It was also one factor which contributed to healthcare costs rising over sixty percent in the following years."

"I should remind you, Senator, that the passage of that legislation provided healthcare to over twenty million Americans that previously had none, and the subsidies provided in the law made it affordable for millions more."

"Members of your party remind us of that every day, Mr. Simon."

"I'm sorry, but your time has expired, Senator," said the Chairman.

The rest of the hearing went pretty much the same way. The Democrats asked benign questions and the Republicans challenged his impartiality and his qualifications. In the end, the Committee voted 14 to 8 to recommend his nomination to the floor. Three days later he was formally approved by the Senate as the new Secretary of HHS.

The following day, Milton and his staff, many of whom worked for him in his congressional office, moved into their new offices at Hubert H. Humphrey building in downtown DC Chris, his chief of staff, retained the position at HHS. Milton was a little overwhelmed as he walked into his large new office and realized he was now overseeing over 80,000 employees of the federal government.

On the other side of town on K street, the pharma lobbyists were celebrating their victory.

"We finally have our own man in place," cheered Nick Price. "Things will be a little easier for at least the next four years."

CHAPTER 34

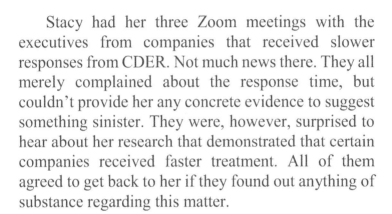

Stacy had her three Zoom meetings with the executives from companies that received slower responses from CDER. Not much news there. They all merely complained about the response time, but couldn't provide her any concrete evidence to suggest something sinister. They were, however, surprised to hear about her research that demonstrated that certain companies received faster treatment. All of them agreed to get back to her if they found out anything of substance regarding this matter.

Stacy continued to follow up with Director Graham, but never got a response. She decided it was time to try and set up meetings with the CEOs of the eight companies that got preferential treatment from the FDA. Unfortunately, only one of the eight would return her calls. Albert Stein had his assistant set up a meet. He wanted to meet her in person. First, to inconvenience her to fly across the country. Second, to face his opponent face to face. He made the appointment for Monday morning so she would have to ruin her weekend flying 3,000 miles west. He didn't realize she didn't have weekends anyway.

Stacy made the most of it. She decided to fly out on Friday night to visit her parents and then fly the rest of the way on Sunday. It was a great way to split up the trip and visit family at the same time on company money.

Late Friday she arrived in Lima. Her parents were waiting for her at the local regional airport. Her Mom was the first to run and hug her.

"It's been so long. You should come home more often."

"I know Mom, I'm just so busy," she replied as her Dad grabbed her away. "Come here, famous reporter Stacy Ogden. Glad you could find time to visit dear old Dad."

"I'm not famous, Dad. I just write for a famous newspaper."

"That makes you famous by association," he replied as he took her hand-held luggage from her. "This way Ms. Ogden, your car is waiting."

The three left the baggage area and walked to the car which was only a minute away in this small airport.

"I can heat up some leftovers if you're hungry," Mom asked they entered the house.

"That would be great. I didn't actually get filled up on the small bag of peanuts they gave me on the flight."

"Okay, why not go up to your room and freshen up while I heat up some food. It will be ready in fifteen."

"Sounds good."

When Stacy got back downstairs, her mother had set up enough food for five people.

"Mom, do you want me to gain twenty pounds?"

"It certainly wouldn't hurt. I wouldn't want to see what's in your refrigerator. Probably a lot of frozen TV dinners."

"I actually eat very healthy. There is a fresh food market right around the corner from my apartment."

"So how did we deserve the pleasure of your company?" her dad asked.

"As I said on the phone, I'm on my way to California for an interview. I'm meeting one of the top CEOs in the country. His name is Albert Stein, and he is the CEO of Trident Pharmaceuticals, probably the largest drug company in the world."

"Why are you interviewing him?" her father interjected.

"I'm investigating some possible corruption in our government. So far I have discovered that a select few pharmaceutical companies get preferential treatment from CDER."

"What's that?" asked her Mom.

"CDER stands for Center for Drug Evaluation and Research. That is the division of the FDA that approves new drugs. I actually met with its Director a few weeks ago."

"So what kind of corruption?"

"Fortunately, all of the FDA's activity is cataloged on a computer service that can be accessed by the public. I did a lot of research on that website and found that a select group of drug companies get much faster response from the CDER than others."

"So what does that prove?" questioned her Dad.

"By itself, it doesn't prove anything. But it does indicate that there may be something behind the scenes happening since these same eight companies have received this preferential treatment for many years. I also discovered that these same eight companies are heavy contributors to certain politicians who are in a position to influence what goes on at the FDA. It would be against the law to favor one company over others if they are receiving it because of some kind of quid pro quo."

214

"And you think this high-powered CEO is going to admit this to you during your meeting?"

"Obviously, not. But I need to give him an opportunity to address my research and I want to see his reactions as I present it."

"You're fooling around in treacherous waters. You better be careful," her Dad admonished.

"Of course I will," she responded as her mind wandered back to the other evening when she thought she was being followed.

The rest of the evening they spent reminiscing about family stuff and Stacy hit the sack at about midnight and fell asleep quickly since it was an hour later her time. For the next couple of days the family enjoyed each other's company and Sunday afternoon came to quickly. Once again Stacy was off to the airport. They hugged goodbye as the cab rolled up and both Mom and Dad in unison said, "Be careful."

"I will. I love you. Bye."

Stacy arrived at Trident at 9:45 a.m. She was a little taken aback by the building's grandeur. The ten-story building was adorned by an exceptionally large Trident sign. The lobby was extremely spacious and had marble floors and walls. She walked up to the reception desk which had four receptionists working. She chose one of them in the middle which seemed to be the only one not talking on their headsets.

"My name is Stacy Ogden. I have an appointment to meet with Mr. Stein."

"Please have seat and I will let him know you are here."

"Thank you," Stacy responded and found a seat about twenty feet away.

About ten minutes later a svelte woman, probably in her mid-thirties, walked up to Stacy. "Are you Ms. Ogden?"

"Yes."

"Mr. Stein can see you now." As they walked by the reception desk she picked up a badge for Stacy. "Please wear this at all times while you are in the building."

"Of course, thank you."

Albert Stein Greeted her with a smile as she entered his ornate office. He was a giant of a man. At least six foot five, he must have weighed 280 pounds. He had a triple chin, big lips, a receding hairline and puffy eyes. But despite his poor appearance he had an air of arrogance and confidence.

"Please come in, Ms. Ogden," he said while motioning to her a seat by a small round conference table in the corner of his office.

"You can remove your mask if you like. I get tested every week and I am fine. Since you were able to fly here, I guess you are too."

"Thank you," she responded as she removed her mask. "I can't wait till we don't have to wear these anymore," she continued.

"You probably won't. Our recently approved vaccine will create the herd immunity we need to get past this."

"Speaking of that vaccine, your company really was able to develop that quickly and get it approved."

"Yes we were, with the help of a fast-tracking process, it was done in less than a year."

"I understand that there were several other companies also developing a similar vaccine, but they weren't able to get as quick a response from the FDA as you were throughout the year."

"I can't speak to that. We are only glad we were able to develop ours so quickly."

"Of course, and in addition to helping eliminate this pandemic it also increased the value of your company by billions."

"That is the reward for hard work and success."

"Unfortunately, the other companies which you were able to beat to the punch will not be rewarded for their hard work."

"Maybe not this time, but who knows on the next one."

"Well, that's why I'm here to see you. I've done a little research regarding the FDA approval process," she continued as she pulled out her spreadsheets. "According to my investigation, there are eight pharmaceutical companies that appear to receive preferential treatment from the CDER. My research shows that over the past ten years the average response time from the CDER for those eight companies is at least twice as fast as for their competitors. Your company is one of those eight. I was wondering if you have any idea why that is the case?" she finished as she handed him the spreadsheets.

"That's very impressive research you have done here. Maybe I should hire you to work for me. As to your question, I'm really not in a position to answer that. I think the FDA might be in a better position to respond."

"I agree, but unfortunately, the key people there are not responding to my inquiries. I thought, since your company has received such fast responses, that you might have a comment for my story."

"My only comment is that we are grateful for the help the FDA has provided us in getting so many important drugs approved for use in our country. I can only surmise that they prioritize both the most important potential drugs and those companies that have a track record of success."

For the next thirty minutes they discussed the current vaccine and a little about the approval process they must go through. Stacy thanked him for his time and headed back off to the airport. Without traffic, she might be able to catch an earlier flight and get home tonight instead of having to catch the red eye.

Back in Washington, Grace was opening a Fedex package that had just arrived for Director Graham. It was two first class plane tickets to Hawaii with a note that read "From your friends at Dartpong, LLC." *What a weird name* she thought. She placed them on top of today's mail and put them on the Director's desk. The Director had left to use the rest room and left his phone behind. While placing the mail she heard the beep of an incoming text. It was from Albert Stein and read "Just met with Stacy Ogden. Potential bad news. Continue to avoid."Grace quickly left when she heard the Director coming. "I just placed the mail on your desk, Dr. Graham."

"Thank you, Grace," he responded as he entered his office.

Grace had her suspicions about some improper activity here at CDER, but she didn't have anything concrete. She and the other executive assistants had discussed it before but decided they should just keep their mouthes shut. After all, they didn't have any real evidence and why risk a good government job? Now, for the first time, she had something tangible. She wondered if she should do anything about it.

CHAPTER 35

When Stacy's jet touch downed at La Guardia airport a text was waiting for her. It was from an unknown number. It read, "We need to talk. I have something for you. This is Grace Winsten from CDER."

It was very late, so Stacy decided to wait until the next day to get back with Grace. She also wanted to talk with her editor about what she has uncovered so far and get his take on how to deal with Grace. Despite the jet lag, Stacy was up early the next morning and was in the office by eight. Martin Grimes was already in his office, too.

"Martin, do you have a minute?" asked Stacy as she approached his door.

"Sure, come on in."

Stacy filled him on her investigation and showed him the text from Grace. "This might be the smoking gun we have been looking for," she said.

Martin took a second to look at the text and consider its importance. "I think we may have something here, Stacy."

"How do you propose I handle this?"

"It might be best for you to meet with her privately first, so she doesn't get overwhelmed. See what evidence she has for you. If it is conclusive then you can set up a time for her to come into our offices to get whatever she has on the record."

"That makes sense. I'll get on it right away," she replied as she left his office.

"Please close the door on your way out and keep me updated on your progress."

As soon as the door was closed, Martin pulled out a cell phone from his desk drawer. He dialed a one button call and waited for the answer. "It's five-thirty in the morning here, what's the emergency?"

"You have a problem."

Back at her desk Stacy sent a reply to Grace's text – "When can we talk?"

A reply came back quickly – "Tonight, Outback Steakhouse bar in Silver Springs, 7 p.m."

"See you there," Stacy wrote back. She was certainly racking up the frequent flyer points. She booked the New York to Washington shuttle which left at two p.m. She didn't want to be late. This gave her a few hours to follow up on other issues. She wanted to meet with the new Secretary of HHS. To her surprise, although she wasn't able to see him, she was able to wrangle a meeting with his chief of staff. She said she would be in Washington tonight and could meet tomorrow anytime. They agreed to an 11 a.m. meeting. On the way out she went by Martin's office and brought him up to date.

Stacy arrived on time in DC She took a cab to her hotel, checked in, and took a short nap to try and catch up on her sleep, which had been severely deprived over the past couple of weeks. She set the alarm for six o'clock Unfortunately, she couldn't fall asleep as her mind kept re-hashing all she learned and wondered what Grace could provide. She watched the alarm clock on the nightstand go from four to five and finally gave up at five thirty and turned off the alarm and got up.

She took a shower and had to put the same clothes back on, since she didn't have time to retrieve fresh ones from her apartment on the way to La Guardia. She took some time to review her notes, especially the ones from her initial interview with Director Graham. She put some fresh make-up on and left for the restaurant. She walked straight there and arrived early enough to have a cocktail before Grace was to arrive. She didn't notice a man with a Giants cap sitting alone in a brown sedan near the parking lot entrance.

At about ten minutes to seven, Grace walked through the front door and walked toward the bar, which by then was pretty full. She noticed Stacy at the corner guarding the empty seat next to her and walked straight to her.

"Hello, Ms. Ogden," she said nervously.

"Hello, Grace. Please call me Stacy. Thank you for contacting me. Can I get you a drink?"

"Yes, I think that would be good."

Stacy called the bartender over. "What can I get you?"

"I'll take a Tom Collins," Grace replied.

"Coming right up."

Stacy decided to go easy with Grace and just did small talk until her drink arrived. She didn't want to spook her and thought a few sips of alcohol would settle her down, since she was obviously very stressed.

Eventually, Stacy asked, "So what did you want to share with me?"

"I've worked at the CDER for over twenty years. For the last five years I have worked for Director Graham.

During that time I have noticed that it appeared that we gave some companies better treatment than others."

"In what way?" Stacy interjected.

"Well, I would note that the Director responded to personal calls from these favored companies and basically ignored calls from others. A few times I heard him give instructions to subordinates that could be construed to help his favorite companies and possible delay help to others. A few of us at CDER would occasionally talk about this, but we had no concrete evidence to support our theory. Of course, we were concerned about retribution if we said anything."

"What's changed?"

"Yesterday, I mistakenly opened a Fedex package that was labeled Confidential and gave it to Director Graham with the rest of the mail. Inside the envelope were two first class tickets to Hawaii with a note that read 'From your friends at Dartpong, LLC'. I thought that was a really weird name and tried to remember if I had heard it before."

"Had you?"

"No, and I don't know why I started to think more about it on the way home, but I think I figured out what it stands for. The first letter of the Director's favorite companies – D for Dickenson Drugs, A for

Allen Labs, R for Rocko Pharmaceuticals, T for Trident Pharmaceuticals, P for Progressive Labs, O for Omni Drugs, N for Nexus Labs and G for Grantham Pharmaceuticals."

"Wow, that's incredible thinking. So you believe that these companies have been, in effect, bribing Director Graham to get favorable treatment."

"Unfortunately, I do. And there's more. While I was dropping off the mail to the Director's desk, a message came in on his cell phone. It was from Albert Stein and it was about you."

"Really. What did it say?"

"I wrote it down right away so I wouldn't forget it. It said 'Just met with Stacy Ogden. Potential bad news. Continue to avoid'."

"Wow, I didn't realize that I was that popular."

"That text doesn't sound like you are that popular?"

"True. This information is immensely helpful, but are you willing to come forward now?"

"I think it's time."

"Obviously, you may not last long at the agency once you've come forward. In the meantime, and before we go public with this information do you think you can find some more incriminating evidence?"

"I can try. I might be able to access the Director's emails and see if there is anything else there."

"You'll have to be incredibly careful and don't tell anybody else about this. I would like to fly you to New York next week to meet with my editor and solidify this evidence. I'll keep in touch with you in the meantime."

"Okay, I'll wait for your call. Please only reach out to me after hours."

"I understand," Stacy said as she paid the drink bill.

The two ladies left and said their goodbyes as Stacy started walking back to her hotel. Grace started her engine and started her drive home. The drive should have only taken about ten minutes, but a construction detour took her the long way home around the hills of Colonial Village. As she began her descent from the top of the hill she noticed something unusual about her brakes. As she applied them harder something snapped and the car started to accelerate as she rolled down the hill. It continued to gather speed as she descended. She did her best to keep the car on the road, but as it reached about sixty down the curvy asphalt, she finally lost control and the car careened over the guard rails and into Rock Creek. She was dead on impact.

Stacy couldn't wait to tell her boss what she had uncovered, so she phoned him first thing the next morning before her appointment at HHS. She conveyed the conversation with Grace and he commended her good work. He advised her that she would have to have Grace come to New York to codify her story. He was intrigued by the Dartpong, LLC portion and told her to keep him posted about what she found out.

She took a shower and put on the same clothes for the third time. She vowed to throw them away when she got home. After a quick cup of coffee in the lobby, she grabbed a cab to the Hubert H. Humphrey Building. After a short wait, she was escorted to her meeting with Bart Kingston.

Bart was a tall, devilishly handsome man even though he was obviously in his 60s with stylish silver hair. When he smiled to greet Stacy, his dimples made him look much younger and even more handsome, if that was possible. Stacy almost forgot why she was here. *With those looks he probably could get away with murder*, she thought.

"Thank you for taking time to meet me," Stacy started.

"My pleasure. What can I do for you?"

Stacy decided to get right to the point. "I have been investigating some activity regarding the FDA and since your boss is basically in charge of that agency, I wanted to get some comments about my research."

"What kind of activity?"

"It appears that for the past ten years certain pharmaceutical companies have received preferential treatment from the FDA," she said as she handed him copies of her spreadsheets. "I have also recently discovered that these same companies may have been bribing high ranking officials at the agency."

"That certainly would be unethical if not illegal," Bart commented.

"Of course, and that is why I think this needs to be investigated. Have you heard anything like this before?"

"Well, as I'm sure you know, my boss only recently took over this position, so we really haven't had a chance to review all of our agency activity, but I appreciate you bringing this to our attention. I'm sure the Secretary will be taking a hard look at this. If you could provide me the information about the alleged bribery, I can assure you we will look into forthright."

"Of course I will be glad to at the appropriate time. But I also did some research regarding these preferred companies and discovered that they had made exceptionally large contributions to certain candidates who had oversight of the agency. Your boss happened to be one who received the most significant support. I wonder if you or he would like to comment on this?"

Bart took a minute to consider her question and replied, "I'm sure many members of the pharmaceutical industry, and all others for that matter, make contributions to political candidates. Obviously, each industry may focus their support on candidates that have influence in their space. That support is given based on the knowledge they have about the candidate's already confirmed positions on important matters to them. And as I'm sure you know that support is not limited to one candidate or party."

"I understand that; however, it is interesting that the same eight companies continually receive preferential treatment from an important agency and the same eight companies are the largest contributors to elected officials that oversee that agency. And, of course, there are the bribes I previously mentioned."

"I can assure you that the Secretary would never condone such a thing. When you can provide me evidence of this we will definitely investigate and take proper actions."

"Glad to hear that, but in the meantime, would you like to comment on my query about the political contributions?"

"I would only say that Secretary Simon has never used his influence to directly benefit any supporter either in his short tenure here at HHS or previously when he served in Congress and he never will. Is there anything else?" he said curtly.

"No, I think that about does it. Thank you again for your time."

"Thank you for bringing some of these items to our attention. I look forward to receiving the additional evidence you discussed. I will advise the Secretary about them. Let me escort you to the lobby."

Well, that's exactly what I expected him to say, Stacy thought as she exited the building. She hailed a taxi and caught the next flight back to New York. She couldn't wait to change clothes. Upon arriving back at New York, she decided to spend the rest of the day working from home. Her first matter of business was to research Dartpong, LLC. *That was brilliant of Grace to uncover the meaning of that name. Not sure I would have ever realized that.*

She started by investigating the company's jurisdiction. Apparently it was formed in Nevada, famous for its anonymity provisions and the fact it had no corporate state tax. Although the public records showed the officers, it did not indicate who actually owned the company. It also listed the registered agent. She started there. Of course, that was a dead end since the registered agent was merely a person with three hundred mailboxes who served in that capacity for all kinds of companies and had little, or no, contact with the company.

The company's president and sole officer ended up being more interesting. It was an attorney at Madison Walsh, Milton Simon's old firm. She wrote down the limited contact information and called him immediately, since he was three hours behind her on the west coast.

"Madison Walsh, how can I direct your call," the receptionist answered.

"I'd like to speak with Andrew Weiss, please."

"Please hold, I'll put you through."

After a few seconds a woman answered and said, "This is Mr. Weiss' office. How may I help you?"

"Hello, my name is Stacy Ogden, I am a reporter with the *New York Times,* and I would like to speak with Mr. Weiss if he is available?"

"May I tell him what this is in reference to?"

"I'm calling about Dartpong, LLC. I was hoping he could give me some color for a story I am writing."

"Let me see if he is available," she responded.

"After quite a few minutes she came back on the line and said, "I'm afraid he is not available at this time. Can I take your telephone number and have him return the call?"

Stacy was used to getting stonewalled and decided to just leave her number. "Please have him call as soon as possible. I am almost finished with my story and wanted him to have an opportunity to respond before I submit it for publication," she added, hoping it would motivate him to call.

So she had an inkling about who owned the company, but couldn't confirm it. The registered agent was a dead end and the sole officer of the company wouldn't talk to her. The financial information was completely unavailable. But there was one other publicly available source to look at – the federal election contribution filings. Stacy had never investigated the various laws regarding political contributions before, so she had to start with the basics.

Now that everything was so easily found on the internet her research went quickly. She confirmed that a popular mechanism for political activity was the political action committee (PAC), which can raise and spend limited "hard" money contributions for the express purpose of electing or defeating candidates. Organizations that raise soft money for issue advocacy were also allowed to set up a PAC. A PAC can give $5,000 to a candidate per election (primary, general or special) and up to $15,000 annually to a national political party. PACs may receive up to $5,000 from any one individual.

On the other hand, a 527 group is a tax-exempt group organized under section 527 of the Internal Revenue Code to raise money for political activities. These groups are typically parties, candidates, committees or associations organized for the purpose of influencing an issue, policy, appointment or election, be it federal, state or local. Such organizations can raise unlimited funds from individuals, corporations or labor unions, but they must register with the IRS and disclose their contributions and expenditures.

A Hybrid PAC, also called a Carey Committee, is a hybrid political action committee that is not affiliated with a candidate and has the ability to operate both as a traditional PAC, contributing funds to a candidate's committee, and as a Super PAC, which makes independent expenditures. The committee can collect unlimited contributions from almost any source for its independent expenditure account, but may not use those funds for its traditional PAC contributions.

Fortunately for Stacy, the Federal Election Committee has a public website that permitted her to search for contributions made to candidates and political action committees. It didn't take her long to uncover that Dartpong, LLC had made millions in contributions to a certain Super PAC called Health for America, as well as maximum contributions to several congressional candidates. The story was finally fitting together, but she just needed a smoking gun. Maybe, just maybe, Grace had what she needed.

CHAPTER 36

Back in Amsterdam, Chris' clinic was a rousing success. They were booked to capacity and had a three-month waiting list. Even celebrities from the U.S. were sharing private jets to reduce their carbon footprint and get The Procedure. None of the patients had exhibited any side effects and all of them reported feeling wonderful. It was too early to see the anti-aging signs, but Chris was confident that it would become apparent soon.

The Procedure started to get major news coverage, first in the EU and then some American press began writing about it. As usual there were some skeptics, but over time as more and more positive testimonials came forward, the coverage was almost universally favorable. In fact, the reporting was so positive that people in the U.S. started clamoring for its approval by the FDA so Cummings Clinic could open back in the States.

In several interviews, Chris had mentioned that he and his team were anxious to come home, but had to wait for the CDER to approve their application. They had enjoyed their time in Europe and they certainly appreciated the cooperation they had received from the EMA, but the U.S. was home. Fox Business News ran a feature story on The Procedure and publicly questioned why the FDA was so slow in approving this groundbreaking therapy, which also prevented people from contracting Covid-19.

Director Graham was feeling the heat. He called Stein and asked for a meeting to discuss how they should handle the uproar. Stein agreed to a meet, but wanted it somewhere off campus where they could not be seen together. They agreed to meet in Middleton, Vermont, a quaint college town in the center of the state. Stein invited Milton to join them, along with a couple of other Dartpong colleagues.

They all met for dinner the following Tuesday at a private dining room at the Middlebury Inn. It wasn't an easy place to get to, but was far enough out of the way that no one would see them. They had to fly into Burlington and drive north about forty-five minutes. The Inn was located right in the middle of town on the roundabout next to the Presbyterian church.

After ordering, Stein called the meeting to order.

"Gentlemen, as I'm sure you've noticed, Chris Cummings therapy has been getting a lot of favorable press lately. The FDA is under extreme pressure to approve it, especially since the EMA did several months ago and all the results seem to be positive. Our esteemed FDA Director feels that we have to do something, so we are here to discuss our options."

237

"Yes," the Director interjected. "If we don't act soon, we may be accused of purposely delaying its approval, which could lead to an investigation that might result in uncovering other issues."

Everyone nodded their heads in agreement.

"Of course," Stein continued, "this could ultimately have a catastrophic impact on our businesses. Consequently, we need to have a plan to make sure this doesn't happen."

"Do you have such a plan, Albert?' one of his colleagues asked.

"I do. Director Graham can proceed with announcing an approval. It will take a few months for it to be finalized and for Cummings to open a clinic back in the States. During that time, we will use our media contacts to promote stories suggesting that this therapy should not be owned by one company that can only perform ten procedures a day. The Procedure should be granted to several large pharmaceutical companies that have the resources to perform literally millions of operations a year so that everyone can ultimately be prevented from further disease."

"But it's so expensive and it would have to continue to be expensive in order for us to make up for lost revenues on our existing business. How will people be able to afford it?"

"Of course, we will have the government pay for it. We can use the current pandemic as a reason for the government's participation. It will be less costly than the trillions the government gave away during the current virus and will prevent it from happening again. Milton, you will have to spearhead this media campaign and, of course, suggest the need for the government's contribution."

"I understand and fully support your position," replied Milton.

"But once people stop getting sick, what will our companies do?" questioned another colleague.

"We will make more money off this program than we would make in twenty years with our current business. We can live off the interest for the next century. Even with The Procedure we won't live that long," Stein responded.

"But what if Cummings doesn't cooperate? What if he refuses to turn over his research?"

"Then we employ Plan B."

The following day, Director Graham announced that the CDER staff had recommended approval of the Cummings Procedure and expected the FDA to provide formal approval within the next few weeks.

CHAPTER 37

Stacy, armed with all her research, set off for her meeting with her editor.

"Come in, Stacy," Martin Grimes said as she approached his open door. "Looks like we've got a lot to talk about."

Stacy filled him in on all she had uncovered – Grace's story, Dartpong, LLC, the Super PAC, the contributions to various congresspersons, the FDA favoritism, and the stonewalling from all the pharma companies.

"Very impressive and great work, Stacy," Grimes responded. "Of course, without Grace we have no real story, just a lot of potential circumstantial evidence and conjecture."

"I realize that. I will arrange to have her flown here to get her story and any other evidence she was able to find on the record."

"Perfect. Let me know when she will arrive, and I'll set aside time to meet with her. I'm looking forward to that." *Not in this lifetime*, he thought.

Stacy picked up her research and left the office to call Grace. Back at her desk she texted Grace's private cell, but got no response. She knew she wasn't supposed to call her during working hours so she decided to make a call to Director Graham as a guise to reaching Grace. She called the CDER and asked to speak to Director Graham. Once she was put through to his office a strange voice asked her how she could help.

"This is Stacy Ogden at the *New York Times*. I'm calling for Director Graham."

"I'm sorry, but he is in a meeting. Can I take a message?"

"No, that's okay, I'll try later. By the way, I have talked with Director Graham a few times and his office phone was always answered by someone else, I think her name was Grace."

"Oh, of course you probably haven't heard, but Grace died in a car accident last week. Everyone here was quite shocked and dismayed. She was well liked."

Stacy tried to remain calm while her insides were churning. "When exactly did this happen?"

"Three nights ago. Apparently she had too much to drink at a local restaurant and drove off the road on her way home."

Stacy just hung up the phone. *Obviously, she had not had too much to drink. She only drank half of a weak Tom Collins. But how did they find out about Grace?*

She had no choice but to bring the bad news to Grimes.

"I know for sure she was not drunk when she left me. This must be even bigger than we thought. Should we call the police?"

"Stacy, so far we only have speculation about any of this, nothing concrete. Nothing you could say to the police will be helpful to their investigation, and we lose a potential scoop by making all of this public now. You need to keep digging and see if you can find something definitive."

"I just don't know where else to look. Everybody is just shutting me out."

"You're a great reporter, you'll come up with something. Just keep me informed of your progress."

Stacy was crestfallen. She felt responsible for Grace's death and she had no real evidence to support her story or to help find Grace's killer. Sally Richardson, a beat reporter a couple of desks down, noticed Stacy's forlorn look.

"Stacy, are you alright?" she asked.

Stacy could hardly answer. "Not really."

"Look, its lunch time. Let's grab something together and let me be a soundboard. Maybe have a glass of wine, too."

"I'm not sure."

"Oh, come on. We haven't talked in weeks. You can fill me in on this hush hush investigation you've been working on."

"Okay, I guess I could use some company and somebody's shoulder to cry on."

The two girls walked to the café on the corner. Stacy told her everything, including her guilt about Grace.

"That's an incredible story. I can't believe that Grimes doesn't think you have enough to go public with."

"You know how cautious the legal department is about having all the T's crossed and I's dotted before publishing anything. I just can't figure out where to go from here. None of the real players will even talk to me. Most of the legal documents are protected by state laws and I can't get access to any financial records except the contributions from the FEC."

"I think I know someone who might be able to help."

"Really?"

"My boyfriend does a little hacking on the side. Maybe he can access some information for you."

"What! Are you kidding? Wouldn't that be illegal?"

"When you're swimming with sharks you have to behave like one," she replied.

"I'm not sure about that."

"Stacy... what else can you do? Just meet with him and see what he might be able to do. He's coming to my apartment for dinner tonight. You can meet him there."

"Alright, it can't hurt to just meet him."

"Great, here's the address, come on over at about seven."

The girls finished their lunch and walked back to work. Stacy spent the rest of the afternoon collating all her research and trying to figure out what her next step could be. She knew something was there, she just couldn't prove it, yet.

Stacy arrived at Sally's apartment just after seven. "Come on in Stacy, meet Tommy. Tommy, this is Stacy, one of our top reporters at the *Times*." They all took a seat in her small living room. "I've given Tommy a little background, but not the details."

Stacy decided Tommy should know all the details if he were going to get involved, so she shared everything with him.

"I don't know if it would be right for you to try and hack your way into some information. It might get you in trouble or even worse, these people could come after you," Stacy warned.

"You don't have to worry about that. A good hacker leaves no trail. I might be able to uncover some financial records, but the ownership information about a Nevada LLC will not be available. That information is not submitted to anyone, so there is likely no data to hack anywhere."

"What about from the law firm that set up the company?"

"You know who they are?"

"Yes."

"Well, that would make it easy. Law firms don't have nearly the cyber security arrangements than the government or financial institutions do."

"You're sure you want to do this?" Stacy asked.

"No problem, anything for a friend of Sally's. I need to brush up on my hacking skills anyway."

They spent the next hour going over more details about her investigation and Tommy agreed to spend some time over the next week hacking, where possible, into the FDA, the Madison Walsh law firm and any financial transactions by Dartpong.

"Thank you so much for your help. Let me let you guys enjoy what's left of the evening," Stacy offered as she grabbed her coat and left.

Stacy was going to bring Grimes up to date on her efforts, but thought it might be better to wait and see if they came up with anything meaningful. She also wasn't sure if he would think hacking was a good investigative procedure.

CHAPTER 38

"We're going home!" Chris yelled across the office after he received word of the FDA's approval. Everyone looked up to see what the commotion was all about.

"The FDA has just approved our Procedure. We are going home. I'd like to give all of you the rest of the day off, but there are patients waiting for their treatment, so I guess the party starts at 6 p.m."

The whole office erupted in applause and cheers. It had truly been a long journey and it was about to end. Of course, they didn't realize this was really the beginning of the end.

Chris and Susan began plans immediately to close the Amsterdam clinic and open a new one back home. It was an exciting time for them, a new beginning. It would take a few months to finish the treatments for those on the waiting list and they would leave behind a skeletal staff to handle follow-up visits. Not that anyone needed these visits, since

there had been no adverse reactions, but the team wanted to create updated data on the anti-aging results.

Not long after the FDA formal announcement, a few unflattering social media posts began to show up. They suggested that The Procedure was too important a discovery to be available for only rich people, especially during the current pandemic. In the beginning these posts did not get much attention, but eventually the topic gained traction. By the time Chris had set up his new clinic in Silicon Valley, a larger group of posters were demanding that it be provided for everybody.

Before too long, the mainstream media picked up the story. CNN interviewed the congressman from Arizona, who suggested that preventing everyone from getting The Procedure was actually racist, since African Americans, by and large, could not afford the treatment. MSNBC had multiple segments where similar theories were espoused.

Chris finally had to agree to an interview to defend himself and his company. He agreed to be interviewed by *60 Minutes*. The interview started okay, as he was asked to explain The Procedure and its benefits. But eventually, he was asked about its costly price.

He was prepared.

"My family and staff sacrificed for many years to develop this important therapy. I invested my life's savings and a few angel investors invested millions to get us to where we are today. Once we finished The

248

Procedure's development, we met with counsel to determine the best way to protect our investment. The only sure way to protect it, according to them, was to maintain total control over its implementation. So we had to make the difficult decision to perform all of the treatments in-house. I had our CFO run the numbers and come up with the least costly approach that would allow us to recover our investment and provide a reasonable profit for our years of work and sacrifice. I know the cost is high, but the benefits are much greater than, for instance, some plastic surgery procedures that produce temporary results and cost about the same amount. I don't see anyone complaining about those costs."

"I'm not sure it is appropriate to compare eliminating disease with plastic surgery," the interviewer continued.

"Why not?"

"I think that's obvious. But let's not get bogged down in a discussion about analogies. Many people have suggested that not providing The Procedure to the masses is really racist, since most African Americans cannot afford it. How do you respond to that criticism?"

"First, I understand that most Americans, at this time, cannot afford The Procedure, not just blacks. But they also can't afford Ferraris. Does that mean that the Italian car maker is racist as well?"

"You seem to like to rely on inappropriate analogies to defend yourself. Having a particular car and having good health are two completely different issues."

"I'm sorry, but the issue here isn't about cars or health or plastic surgery. The issue is about whether I have the right to do with my own property what I please. I purposely did not accept any help or grants from the government so that I would not be beholden to them in the future. I only ask that people understand and agree that what I and my staff and investors created is ours to do with what we want."

"I'm not sure most people would agree with you on that point, but we appreciate the time you took to explain your position."

That interview created a media storm. Most of the coverage portrayed Chris as a greedy businessman, only interested in his own well-being. A few on social media supported him and agreed he had the right to do anything he wanted with the discovery he made and paid for. Many called for the government to step in. The Health for America Super PAC suggested that the government force Chris to provide his research to large pharmaceutical companies that had the resources to offer The Procedure at a much lower cost. For those who couldn't afford it, the government could subsidize those treatments.

Several more conservative outlets gave tacit support to Chris. They wrote articles agreeing with his private property theory, but suggested he should consider some alternatives that would allow more people to receive the treatment.

Chris agreed to be interviewed by CNBC, even though the last one didn't go so well. He felt the need to get exposure for his side of the story and thought a business network would be more receptive to his position. Obviously, he didn't do his homework.

The interview started, as did the *60 Minutes* one, by applauding him for his discovery. It quickly moved to why he was limiting the number of patients who could receive the treatment. Chris reiterated the positions he had offered on the previous interview.

"If you are wanting to make sure you are adequately compensated for your investment and efforts, why not sell it to big pharma?" the interviewer asked.

"First, I haven't had an offer. Second, what would be the right price? Would a therapy that eliminates disease and slows the aging process by forty percent be worth more than an iPhone? I guess an appropriate price would be about two trillion dollars, since that is Apple's valuation today."

"No one would be able to pay that price."

"Exactly, that is why they haven't made an offer. They would just prefer to steal it. Lobbyists cost a lot less."

"Are you suggesting that big pharma will collude with the government to take over your property without properly compensating you for it? That is an outlandish allegation."

"I'm not making any allegations. I'm only trying to protect my own property and provide value to those who find my therapy worth its cost."

"But what about those who can't afford the cost?"

"What about them? They are in the exact same position they were before I made my discovery. No better, no worse."

"But they could be better."

"They could be better if they all lived in mansions, drove expensive sports cars, and dined at fancy restaurants every night, but of course, that is not reasonable to expect."

"That's not the same."

"Why not?"

"I'm sorry our time is up, but we thank you for joining us today. We'll be back after this short break."

CHAPTER 39

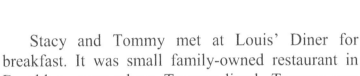

Stacy and Tommy met at Louis' Diner for breakfast. It was small family-owned restaurant in Brooklyn, near where Tommy lived. Tommy was already sitting in the corner booth when Stacy arrived. As Stacy sat she said, "I can't believe you were able to hack into all these places so fast."

"I've been doing this since I was a kid. People don't realize how easy it is to break cyber security. Foreign countries hack our most secure data all the time. Even our own country hacks information from around the world and even its own citizens. There will never be real privacy again. If you don't want somebody to know something about you, don't use any device connected to the internet to share it," Tommy replied.

"That's scary. So what did you find out?"

"Quite a lot. First, you were almost right about the LLC ownership. It is not owned by the corporations, but rather their CEOs. Albert Stein owns thirty percent and the other seven own ten percent each. The company was formed in Nevada in 2005 with only one million dollars. About a month later they set up an offshore subsidiary in Cayman to avoid U.S. taxes.

The investments are made from that entity which is managed by someone you may have heard of."

"Who?"

"Theodore Simon."

The father of Milton Simon?"

"None other."

"The plot begins to thicken."

"Yes, it does. The company is now worth over fifty million dollars, even though they have made tens of millions in contributions."

"How is that possible?"

"Really good investments. Most of the time the assets are held in a diversified group of blue-chip stocks and bonds. But once or twice a year the fund makes a big option play which produces huge gains. They always seem to time the market perfectly and never have a loss."

"Can you explain to me how those options work?"

"Yeah, if you're not familiar with them they can be a little confusing. There are basically two types of options – puts and calls. A put option allows you to sell stock to someone else at a particular price. Hedge funds typically buy put options on stocks they own, so that if it falls dramatically, they have a guaranteed buyer at a predetermined price. But some people buy naked put options, that's when they don't own the stock, to gamble that the stock price is going to fall. If it falls, they can then buy the stock at the new lower price and sell it at the predetermined put option price and profit on the falling stock price. Call options are the exact opposite. Call options give you the right to buy stock at a predetermined price. So if you think a stock is going to rise in price, then you can buy call options and profit when the stock rises. The options cost a fraction of the price of the stock so you can leverage your gains by buying options instead of the actual stock."

"Why doesn't everybody just buy options if they cost less and the gains can be larger and just wait for the stock to move in the right direction?"

"That's because options expire after a certain period of time. So if you buy options, you have to be right about the price movement and the timing. If you're wrong on either, you can lose all your money. Buying options is a riskier trade."

"I see. But the Dartpong people always seem to get both right all the time?"

"They only make one or two trades a year, but they have always been right."

"What kind of companies do they trade in?"

"Here's the interesting part. With few exceptions they only make option trades in pharmaceutical companies. And because these trades are made through multiple offshore accounts, they haven't ever been flagged as potential inside trading moves."

"And you say that Theodore Simon is responsible for all the investment decisions?"

"He is named as the account manager and he receives substantial advisory fees for his services."

"What's substantial?"

"Over the past fifteen years I would say about twenty million dollars."

"Wow!"

"And it was actually he who bought the first-class plane tickets for Director Graham at the FDA."

"Well, that makes sense. They wouldn't want to have a direct link to Dartpong. But let's go back to the trades for a minute. Did you make a list of the option trades and the dates they were made?"

"Yes, I created a spreadsheet which I can email you. I looked up a couple of them myself, and I think you will find them interesting."

"Did you find out anything else?"

"One more weird piece of data. There is someone named Peter Junkin named as a sub-advisor on one of the offshore accounts who receives $10,000 a month in payments. I did some checking on him and he lives in a middle-income neighborhood outside of Washington D.C. and doesn't appear to have any financial experience. He lives with his wife who apparently has some kind of debilitating illness."

"That is weird. I wonder why he receives those payments if they're not for financial advice?"

"Based on what we've uncovered so far, my guess is not for a good one. That's all I have so far, but I'm going to try and hack into cell phone records and see if they shine any more light on all of this."

"Thanks Tommy, you have really done enough already. I really appreciate your help with this."

They finished breakfast with small talk, mostly about their common friend Sally. Stacy paid the check and as they left they paid no attention to the man wearing a Giants baseball cap who followed them out the door.

Stacy waved goodbye and caught a taxi to the office back in Manhattan. She decided to research the trades from the spreadsheet Tommy had sent her. She wanted to have all her ducks in a row before showing everything to Martin Grimes.

What she uncovered from the trades was just what she was looking for. Every time the offshore entity bought puts, within a few days the FDA turned down an application for a new drug from the company on which they had bought the puts. This caused the shares to plummet and Dartpong made a fortune. On the other hand, every time they bought call options on a drug company, the FDA within a few days, or sometimes a couple of weeks, approved one of their applications. Of course, those companies' stock rose on the news and as a result Dartpong made a fortune on those trades, as well. The only exception was a trade they made on the whole market in February of 2020. Near the middle of the month, they bought a huge amount of puts on the S&P 500 index. Less than a month later the market cratered on news of the pandemic and Dartpong made a $15,000,000 profit on the puts.

Stacy had a lot of evidence to make her case, but she was unsure how the paper would think about her methods of getting it. She certainly couldn't reveal her source for the information. She didn't want to endanger another person.

As she was gathering all the materials together to show Grimes, Sally came up to her and asked, "Did you meet with Tommy this morning?"

"Yes, he did a fantastic job. I wanted to thank you for putting us together."

"Do you know where he was going after you met?"

"No, why?"

"I can't reach him. He always has his cell phone with him and he doesn't answer. I've called him about ten times."

"Maybe he is on another call and can't take yours."

"For three hours?"

"I don't know what to say. He was fine when he left me," Stacy offered, but she too had a bad feeling. *I hope this is not another Grace situation. How could they know about him?*

CHAPTER 40

2022

The emergency room at Walter Reed Medical Center was filling up quickly, as were several other hospitals around Washington. All the new patients had the same symptoms as Milton Simon – trouble breathing, elevated blood pressure, and seizures, but no known cause.

Dr. Reed ordered the medical histories on all the patients to see if he could find a common denominator. When they finally arrived, he found one. All the patients had recently had The Procedure performed. This was even more puzzling, since all the data over the past couple of years showed no adverse effects from the treatment. In fact, it appeared that the therapy was extremely beneficial for everyone who received it.

He called a meeting of all his colleagues who were attending these patients to brainstorm. Once everyone was gathered in the hospital's conference room, he advised them of the information he had discovered from the patient histories. The attendant who had first seen Simon Milton offered, "I did hear Secretary Milton say that we should try to get in touch with Dr. Chris Cummings. I'm sure you know it was his firm that discovered this therapy and until recently only his clinic administered it."

"That is certainly our best, and what appears to be our only, course of action. Have the admitting office try to reach him immediately," replied Dr. Reed. "In the meantime, run all the tests you can think of and try to keep the patients as comfortable as possible."

As more and more patients came in, they had to set up temporary triages. The emergency room was already filled to capacity. Dr. Reed finally ran into the admitting office himself.

"Has anyone reached Dr. Cummings, yet?"

"Not yet. It seems nobody knows where he is."

CHAPTER 41

Albert Stein had called Milton and told him it was time to move ahead with their plan. He needed to contact Chris Cummings and explain that it was time to voluntarily transfer his research to eight other companies which would be selected by the FDA, in return for a royalty payment, that would allow them to broadly distribute the therapy to all Americans and eventually the world in a more robust way. The current pandemic required this action, and if he didn't agree, the government might assert its eminent domain authority to confiscate the research. Stein said he would leave it up to him to negotiate the royalty payment, since it didn't matter much to him, since he would be passing the cost onto the government anyway.

Of course, Milton understood that the ultimate eight companies selected would be Stein and his buddies. He realized that he really had no choice and hoped he would be successful in negotiating a deal with Chris. After all, people were still dying because of Covid-19 despite a third of Americans having taken the vaccines, and his therapy could eliminate that.

He asked his assistant to set up an in-person appointment with Chris. He would fly to California, and he could spend some time with his father while he was there. He also was thinking he could get some pointers from him on how to approach Chris.

The meeting was set up for the following week, which was the second week in September. He flew in over the prior weekend and would stay at his parents' house. He arrived mid-afternoon and had a government car pick him up and take him home. His Mom greeted him at the door with open arms. She hadn't seen him, at least in person, for many months.

"Milton, how are you?" she asked as she hugged him.

"I'm fine Mom. Just a long flight."

"Well, come in and freshen up. I'm having the staff make a special dinner for us tonight."

"Thanks Mom. I'm looking forward to a nice home-cooked meal and time with my family."

"Your father should be home in a couple of hours, so why not take a little time to relax? I'll let you know when he gets home."

"That's a great idea," he said as he started climbing the stairs to his old bedroom. He took a quick shower and decided to take a short nap while he waited for his father.

After about an hour nap he was awakened by a rap on his door.

"Are you awake, son?" his father asked through the door.

"I am now," Milton responded.

"Sorry to wake you, but I wanted to let you know I'm home."

"No problem. I'm glad you did. I'll be down in a few minutes."

"Okay, I'll have a drink waiting for you."

Milton redressed and met his father in his office. "So how are things in Washington?" Theodore asked.

"They're fine, it's just a little hectic with this pandemic and all. We all thought the vaccines would end this nightmare, but it may take a little more time before things get back to normal."

"It would get that way a lot sooner if that Cummings therapy was available for everyone," the senior Milton said.

"Sounds like you've been talking to our favorite benefactor."

"You know Albert and I are very close. We've been good friends for a long time. You know we discussed that this kind of approach may be necessary."

"I know. It's just difficult for me since Chris and I have been friends since college. Obviously, I haven't been in touch with him much through the years, but this is not going to be easy. You know he has a point about the research being his property."

"Milton, you have to be thinking about all the people you represent. Sometimes the greater good trumps property rights."

"You're probably right, but that doesn't make it any easier. So how do you think I should approach him?"

"I would start by appealing to his sense of national loyalty. He loves what this country stands for, and I'm sure he has a good heart. Then you can discuss how a reasonable royalty payment will improve his financial rewards. Probably best not to use threats and give him some time to consider all the issues. If he doesn't agree on the spot, let him take time to think about it."

"That sounds like a reasonable approach."

"Okay, now that that's settled, let's join your mom for dinner.

The Simons spent a lovely evening together, and Milton excused himself early since he was three hours ahead of them. He didn't sleep much, with his mind thinking about exactly what he would say to Chris. The next morning his government driver took him to Chris' clinic.

"Well, stranger, it's been a while since I've seen your ugly mug," Chris chided him as he entered his office.

"Too long, brother. How's Susan?"

"She's great. Maybe we can all have lunch after our meeting. Please have a seat. So what brings you all the way here?"

"As I'm sure you've seen, you are getting a lot of coverage about The Procedure. Unfortunately, a lot of that is negative, especially given the current health crisis we are still dealing with. Consequently, I'm getting a lot of pressure from various sources to help solve this problem. Many people have suggested that your therapy may be one solution."

"I'm sure if we could give it to enough people it would, but that just isn't possible."

"Well, that's why I'm here. It has been suggested that if major companies distributed The Procedure, everyone could get the treatment quickly. I know you have not been willing to consider that, but I have an idea that might make sense, and I know you would choose to help if there was a reasonable path to do it."

"I'm not sure I would be open to anything like that, but as a courtesy, based on our long friendship, I will listen."

"The idea is relatively simple. You would transfer your research to several large drug companies that would be selected by the FDA. They would pay you a royalty for every treatment given and, since they could ramp up the delivery so quickly, you would surely make more for yourself and your investors than you would by performing only dozens a week as you are now."

"This is still an expensive treatment. How could most people afford it, even if the price was still at least several thousand?"

"I've already talked to many of our legislators and they are prepared to have the government foot the bill."

"It sounds like an interesting idea, but I still don't like the idea of a few large pharmaceutical companies getting free access to my creation."

"But it wouldn't be free. They would have to pay you a royalty."

"You and I both know they wouldn't be paying it. They will add it to the cost and pass it on to the government, which you said would be footing the bill."

"What difference does it make who's paying for it, as long as you get paid?"

"That is the point, Milton. People and their companies should get rewarded for the value they create, not from what they can steal from others, either by themselves or with the help of their influential contacts in influential places."

"I appreciate your philosophy, but there are millions of people who need what you have. Isn't it more important that they get help?"

"That is the same as asking if it is appropriate to kill the ten people sitting in my lobby if that would save a million people. What is right doesn't change, regardless of the circumstances."

"I knew you would be a hard nut to crack. Will you at least think about it? You're the most creative person I know. Maybe you can devise a plan that will work for everyone and still not violate your principals."

"Okay, I will do that. Now let's go have lunch with Susan."

The three of them enjoyed a nice lunch without any discussion about the therapy, which pleased Milton, since he was glad to avoid the subject. They parted after lunch with Chris promising to get back to him. Milton spent the drive back to the airport anguishing over how Stein would respond to his lack of success.

He wanted to get it over with, so he called him from the car. He gave him all the details of the conversation and waited for his response.

"Okay, it's time to exert some pressure. Leak a story to the press that you offered Cummings a significant royalty in return for his research and he turned it down. Spin it so he comes off as a greedy bastard who doesn't care about everybody else's health. I'm sure Bart can help you with that."

"Understood."

CHAPTER 42

Stacy decided to reply to Tommy's email to see if he would respond that way. She tried not to show her alarm so as not make Sally more upset than she already was. An hour later there was no reply and Tommy had not called Sally.

"Do you think I should go to the police?" Sally asked.

"They won't do anything until a person is missing for at least 24 hours and it's only been a few," Stacy replied.

"But he never doesn't return my calls."

"I know, but there could be several reasons for that. His phone could be dead. He could be in an important meeting. Try not to worry too much for now. I'm sure he will show up soon," she said but thought, *I'm not so sure anymore.*

"If anybody asks, tell them I'm going to Tommy's place to see if he is there."

"Don't worry, I'll cover for you."

When Sally left, Stacy finished putting together all her materials to show Grimes. She called his assistant to see when he had an hour to go over everything. She told her that Grimes wouldn't have an open spot until the end of day, so Stacy agreed to meet with him at five.

She figured with the extra time she might as well start writing her article. *Who knows, I might get a Pulitzer for this, if I live that long.* By the time five o'clock rolled around she had finished about a third of her first draft. She gathered up all her files and marched over to Grimes' office.

"Come on in, Stacy. Sorry I wasn't available sooner."

"No problem, just gave me time to start the actual article."

"So, have you come up with anything more concrete?"

"Yes sir, quite a bit. Here's what we have so far. First, we have evidence that eight particular pharmaceutical companies get preferential treatment at the FDA, while their competitors often have delays in responses from the same agency. Next, we know that these same eight companies have CEOs that own a Nevada LLC called Dartpong. This LLC has contributed significant amounts to a Super PAC called Health for America. This Super PAC has provided significant support to several congresspeople who have voted for legislation beneficial for the drug industry and who, in some cases, have FDA oversight. The LLC also has an offshore subsidiary which basically does its investing there in order to avoid U.S. tax. The subsidiary's trading history shows that they make large option bets once or twice a year, for the most part, on pharmaceutical companies right before the FDA makes a favorable or unfavorable application response. The investments are managed by Theodore Simon, the father of Milton Simon, the Secretary of HHS, who just confirmed that he was trying to strike a deal with Chris Cummings where his research would be turned over to several large pharmaceutical companies. I guess we can guess which ones that would be. We also know that the subsidiary lists a sub-advisor named Peter Junkin, who receives monthly payments of $10,000, but has no financial experience. And lastly, we know that Director Graham's assistant, Grace Winsten, died in an unexplained car accident right after she agreed to provide me important documentation and recorded testimony about what's been going on at the FDA. And now, Sally Richardson's boyfriend, who just helped me gather some of this information, has gone missing."

"That's some really good work, Stacy. Can you tell me how Tommy helped you gather that information?"

"I think you'd rather not know."

"I think the paper's attorneys may want to know before they agree to publish this kind of derogatory information."

"If we tell them how we got it, we don't have to reveal our source, do we?"

"I don't think so."

"Well, Tommy is pretty good with computers and he was able to access some databases that provided us this information."

"In other words, he hacked some private and public computer systems to get it?"

"I guess you could say that," she replied sheepishly.

"I'm not sure the lawyers are going to like that," he replied while shaking his head.

"But all of this is true."

"The data you got illegally is true, but some conclusions you are suggesting are just suppositions. You don't know that Grace's death is connected. You can't prove that any contributions made to elected officials resulted in improper votes or oversight. Since Grace is no longer with us, you can't even prove anything about the airline tickets or the alleged text from Albert Stein. And your law-breaking friend Tommy has only been missing for less than a day. Although all of this is great work, I don't think the attorneys will let us publish without more corroborating evidence. Let me run it up the pole and see what their response is. In the meantime, try to get some corroborating evidence or testimony."

"Like I said before, everybody is stonewalling me, so I'm not sure what else I can get."

"Just keep at it, and I'll get back to you," he replied. Martin Grimes was not about to run anything up the pole.

CHAPTER 43

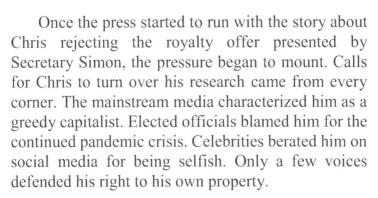

Once the press started to run with the story about Chris rejecting the royalty offer presented by Secretary Simon, the pressure began to mount. Calls for Chris to turn over his research came from every corner. The mainstream media characterized him as a greedy capitalist. Elected officials blamed him for the continued pandemic crisis. Celebrities berated him on social media for being selfish. Only a few voices defended his right to his own property.

Chris stood his ground. He stopped giving video interviews, but continued to respond in writing to news outlet requests for responses to the mounting criticisms. He even agreed to consider selling the research to pharmaceutical companies of his choosing, so long as the payment was appropriate for the benefit received. But that didn't satisfy the critics, especially those that wanted the government to have basic control over any transfer and ultimate use of The Procedure.

Stacy wanted to write a favorable article supporting Chris' position, but Grimes turned down her request, saying that the *Times* didn't want to get in the middle of this fight. He also told her that the attorneys were not prepared to have them publish her article without more corroboration or evidence that had not been obtained through illicit means.

She decided to give Chris a call to let him know some people were on his side. She assumed he was a little disappointed by all the adverse publicity after working so hard to create something so wonderful. She was put through to him immediately by the receptionist.

"Hi Stacy, I wasn't expecting to hear from you."

"I just wanted to call and give you some support."

"Thanks. Things are a little crazy around here. I never thought developing something so beneficial would result in so much hate."

"Me neither. I tried to write an article supporting your position, but it got denied by my editor. The lawyers are also keeping me from writing an article about the pharmaceutical industry and how certain companies are getting preferential treatment from the FDA. I came up with some pretty damning evidence and they still won't go to print with it."

"Sounds like you and I are in the same boat."

"I thought you should know that some of the stuff I discovered indicts your friend Milton Simon."

"Really. I'm not sure I consider him a friend anymore. Can you share the information with me?'

Stacy took the next thirty minutes to share everything with Chris, not just about Milton, but about Dartpong, its subsidiary, the investments, Grace's death, Tommy's disappearance and Milton's father.

"That's incredible. Not that it surprises me. I know you had previously suggested the FDA might be slow playing my application for the benefit of the other drug companies, but I wanted to give them the benefit of the doubt. I should have known better. I actually met Albert Stein many years ago at Theodore Simon's home. He offered me a job right out of college and he ended up buying one of my discoveries, which was what gave me enough money to develop The Procedure."

"He's probably regretting the day he did that."

"Probably. So what are you going to do with all your evidence? Can't you at least turn it over to the authorities?"

"Unfortunately, I didn't exactly get it in a legitimate way. Second, I'm not sure which authorities are not involved in the corruption. It's hard to tell the good guys from the bad ones these days."

"I know. Maybe you could start a blog under an assumed name and get it out on the internet. It might get some others like Grace to come forward."

"I think that is a great idea. The only potential problem is my paper would be able to figure out who's behind the blog."

"So what? So long as they are not on the hook for any libel charges, why would they care? They're still a news organization, they should want to see the truth come out, even if its not in their paper."

"That's true. I think I might just do that. Anyway, I just wanted to give you some moral support and hope things work out for you."

"Thanks, Stacy. I appreciate the call."

Stacy wasn't sure what to do. Grace was dead. Tommy was still missing. She wasn't being allowed to expose the corruption. If she started a blog, maybe the people behind Grace's death and Tommy's disappearance would come after her. In fact, why hadn't they already. She decided there was one more lead she hadn't followed up on, the sub-advisor who live just outside Washington.

She booked the New York – DC shuttle for the next morning. After touchdown, she rented a car and drove out to the address Tommy had given her. He was right, it wasn't an expensive neighborhood. But it was clean and manicured with large trees lining the streets.

When she arrived at the address she saw a white wooden mailbox with the name Junkin on it. This was the place, she thought. Maybe there will be some answers here.

She strode confidently to the front door and rang the bell. A nurse opened the door and asked her what she wanted.

"My name is Stacy Ogden and I'm looking for Peter Junkin. I'm a reporter for the *New York Times* and I wanted a comment from Peter. Is he home?"

"I'm afraid he's not. I think he will be back later today."

"Are you his wife?"

"No, I take care of his wife. She is terribly ill and needs constant attention."

"I'm sorry to hear that. Here is my card, please give it to Peter when he gets home and ask him to give me a call."

"I will," the nurse replied a s she took the card and closed the door.

Stacy decided to do her first stakeout. She parked down the street and waited for Junkin to come home. A few hours later a late model brown sedan drove into the driveway at the Junkin residence. She watched as a middle-aged man got out of the car wearing a Giants baseball cap covering most of his face. She wasn't sure she had seen him before, but there was something familiar about him.

She decided to wait awhile to see if he would call her. After a couple of hours she drove back in front of the house and walked up to the front door. Peter answered the door this time. He had a little shocked look on his face when he saw her. "Can I help you?" he stammered.

"Are you Peter Junkin?" she asked.

"Yes, that's me. Who's asking?" Of course he knew exactly who she was, but wanted to get some time to gather his thoughts and figure out how to handle this situation.

"My name is Stacy Ogden and I am a reporter for the *New York Times*. I'm doing a story about the pharmaceutical industry and wanted to get a comment from you."

"What could I possible contribute to a story about drug companies?"

"Well, as part of my investigation I discovered that some CEOs of eight major pharmaceutical companies own a Nevada LLC called Dartpong and that the LLC has an offshore subsidiary which invests its money."

Drops of sweat began to form on Peter's forehead, but there was no moisture in his throat at all.

"You were listed as a sub-advisor to the subsidiary and apparently have been receiving

$10,000 a month for many years. Could you tell me what you do for that fee?"

The sweat was now actually running down his face. "I'm not sure that that is any of your business," he replied.

"Our research indicates that you have no financial experience, and it seems odd that you would receive significant payments for investment advice when you have no credentials that would merit that."

"I'm sorry, but I have a very sick wife that I need to attend to, and I don't have time to answer questions from reporters," he responded as he closed the door in her face.

That worked out well, she thought as she walked back to her car. *Where have I seen that man before?*

CHAPTER 44

Chris continued to ignore all the calls to give up his research. The pandemic continued to be a problem, even though its affect was diminishing by early 2022. There was still a fear that mutations would cause a rebound of infections, and research to develop further vaccines was under way in several laboratories.

Albert Stein had enough. It was time to implement Plan B. He called for a meeting of his colleagues and required Milton and his father to attend. Once again, they met in an out of the way location to avoid scrutiny. When all the participants had arrived, he called the meeting to order.

"We have given this Cummings guy enough time to agree to our generous terms. He has continued to refuse our offers so now is the time to force the issue."

"How do we do that?" questioned one of his colleagues.

"We do it by Executive Order. In an emergency, the President of the United States can authorize the use of the Stafford Act. For example, in March of last year, President Trump declared a national emergency under the Stafford Act.

"This rule allows the administrator of the Federal Emergency Management Agency to, among other things, to exercise the right of eminent domain to acquire not only the physical facilities it needs, but also supplies like medicine, food, equipment, parts, etc. and to take possession of them immediately."

"I didn't realize the government had that kind of authority."

"Most Americans are unaware that a vast set of laws gives the president greatly enhanced powers during emergencies. There are actually 123 statutory powers that may become available to the president when he declares a national emergency, including the power President Trump invoked to help build the wall," Stein added.

"But what if we can't get the president to sign an Executive Order for us?" another colleague asked.

"If for some reason we can't get the president to sign an Executive Order, Milton, as Secretary of HHS, can determine according to 42 U.S. Code § 1320b–5, after consultation with public health officials as may be necessary, that a disease or disorder presents a public health emergency and take necessary actions to diminish the emergency, including ensuring that sufficient health care items and services are available to meet the needs of individuals," Stein read from his notes. "Of course, it would be better coming from the president, but Milton is our Plan B."

Milton wasn't overly excited about having to step up if the president didn't act. Confiscating his friend's lifelong work didn't appeal to him, but he realized he had no choice if it came to that.

The rest of the meeting was spent discussing who would take what role in contacting the president or his staff regarding the proposed Executive Order. It was decided it was best to use the upcoming holidays as a means to make some informal contacts and they would re-group in January to move forward. Milton left the meeting beginning to wish he stayed a west coast lawyer.

CHAPTER 45

Stacy flew home for the holidays and spent Christmas and New Years with her parents. It gave her a chance to discuss her future plans. She was getting a little disenchanted with her position at the *Times*, given their refusal to publish any part of her investigation or her articles about The Procedure.

She told her parents everything. They had a little bit of mixed emotions about her revelations. They were encouraged by her dogged reporting, but not so excited about some of her methods. And, of course, they were horrified that she might have had anything to do with Grace's death and Tommy's disappearance. They were also concerned about their daughter's well-being.

Stacy admitted she was also uneasy and assured them that she was being cautious. Her bigger concern was about her future. She was no longer happy in her current position. She was thinking about posting her story on the internet, which she felt may result in her dismissal anyway. But then where would she go, what would she do?

"I don't like the idea of you posting this story. These people are dangerous, you don't know how they would respond," her dad admonished.

"Posting it probably is the safest course of action," she replied. "What can they do after its published? If I'm in danger, it is before I post, and they do something to keep me from doing it."

"I can see your point. But what will you do for work?" he replied.

"That's what I'm not sure about. I could go back to work for a small-town paper, or I could just be a freelance writer. I have saved up enough money to support myself while I figure it out."

"Well, of course, your father and I will support any decision you make."

"I know I can count on you both."

Stacy needed a relief from work, so they spent most of the time talking about other things. She left refreshed and ready to conquer the world.

Back in New York, she decided it was time to post her article on the web. She set up two accounts under pseudo names with corresponding email accounts. She used both Facebook and Twitter accounts to reveal her investigative work. She did leave out the information about Peter Junkin, since she had no concrete evidence that he had done something inappropriate and she didn't want to cast aspersions on a potentially innocent person.

She never anticipated what would happen next. Both accounts were almost immediately canceled. She received emails to her new accounts from the social media sites indicating that her accounts had been frozen for 30 days due to the posting of misinformation. She was livid. *How could they know if this information was untrue?* Her requests to both services for further clarification went without response.

As a journalist, she was beside herself. She had spent over six months doing extensive research into this matter, had uncovered what appeared to be a significant conspiracy involving some of the country's biggest corporations and elected officials, maybe even potential murders, and she couldn't publish the information at her own paper or on the web. *What had the world come to?*

CHAPTER 46

Stein had used every source he had to try to convince the president to sign an Executive Order, but without success. He did, however, get him to agree to support Secretary Simon's actions to confiscate the Cummings research on the basis of a national health emergency. He was willing to allow the National Guard to help enforce that action, if necessary.

It was the end of January, a very cold winter in Washington. The streets were full of snow, which was unusual for the Capitol. Stein had flown into Reagan National to meet with Milton and discuss the next steps. They met in the lobby bar at the Jefferson Hotel.

"Secretary Simon, it's your move," said Stein.

"What move?"

"The president has agreed to support your confiscation of the Cummings research based on a national health emergency. He will also provide you the support of the National Guard to accomplish this."

"And when am I supposed to take this action?"

"In three days."

"What about the selection of the companies that will be chosen to provide the treatments?"

"That's already been taken care of. You just need to announce the national emergency and confiscate the research. It's that simple."

I don't know how simple that is, Milton thought.

"Your chief of staff can help you put together the plans which, of course, must be kept quiet until the last minute so Cummings doesn't try to do something stupid, like destroy it." Stein knew Milton probably wouldn't be up to the task himself.

"Are you up to the task, Milton?"

"Of course, sir."

"Okay then, I'll see you on the other side."

Milton didn't want to drive back to Georgetown in this bad weather, so he got a room at the Jefferson. In fact, he didn't want to have contact with his wife until this was over. He was actually nauseous, thinking about what he had to do to a good friend. So he booked the room for three nights.

The next day he met with Bart, his chief of staff, to discuss plans to confiscate the Cummings research. Bart acted like he was hearing about it for the first time, but he had put most of the plans in place already. He let Milton suggest some ideas and then told him he could handle all the details for him. He would draft a statement for him to give the press at a news conference. He assured him he would become a national hero for this. Milton wasn't so sure, but he was glad to turn over the preparations to Bart.

Milton decided to take the afternoon off. He wasn't feeling that well and wanted to be on the top of his game for the press conference tomorrow. His driver took him back to the Jefferson. The snow had stopped falling and the streets were completely clear now, so the ride was only ten minutes. He had some fresh clothes brought from his house.

It was only 3 p.m., but Milton stopped in the lobby bar. He ordered a Makers Mark neat. Then he ordered another one. Since he hadn't eaten anything all day, the alcohol was warming his body and loosening his brain. He picked up his cell phone and made a call. "Crystal, this is Milton."

An hour later Crystal showed up to his suite. She was wearing a tight, short black dress under her fur coat, which she removed as soon as she entered the warm room. Her well-endowed figure was apparent from the low cut of the dress.

Milton was immediately aroused and pulled her to him. The drinks had their full effect by then and he had no patience. She pushed him down on the bed as she demanded that he slow down. He accepted her instructions and watched as she slowly removed her dress. To his delight she was wearing nothing under it and she seductively pranced around the room as Milton hurriedly removed his own clothes.

To her there was no passion, just the fulfillment of an obligation. But Milton was drunk with passion and alcohol, so the sex didn't last long. Within a couple of minutes, he rolled off of her and lay flat on his back with his head propped up on the hotel's fluffy pillows. He just laid there with his eyes glued straight ahead at the ceiling.

"Is something wrong, Milton?" Crystal asked.

"Yes, something is wrong."

"What's the matter?"

Milton hesitated, but ended up telling her what he had to do tomorrow to his good friend. Crystal remembered meeting Chris many years ago. She remembered what a nice guy he was, unlike the asses she was paid to work with on a daily basis. He told her of his hesitance, but he had no choice. She knew exactly how he felt.

A few minutes later Milton was out like a light. Crystal knew what she had to do. She got up and went over to the dresser where Milton's phone was being charged.

She knew his password and opened the contacts page. There it was, Chris Cummings' personal cell number. She took out her own cell phone and sent a message to that number.

She got dressed and left a note for Milton.

"Good luck tomorrow," it read.

CHAPTER 47

Chris' cell phone beeped indicating an incoming message. He read it and immediately found Susan in her office to relay what the message said. They only had one patient left for the day, so they discussed what needed to be done once all the other employees had left. They had been developing a contingency plan for months now, not trusting what the government might do. Both were busy typing and printing out pages they used to replace some of those in a red binder from the office bookshelf. Another couple of pages were enclosed in an envelope which was addressed to their corporate counsel. One last text to send from a burner phone and they were done. By ten o'clock they had finished everything and left the clinic.

The next morning Secretary Simon called a press conference for ten a.m Eastern time. All the major news organizations had set up their microphones inside the HHS building's lobby. Milton had come to the office early to practice his speech. He was still a little hungover from yesterday's binge.

At 10 a.m. sharp he approached the lectern and read from his prepared notes. "Good morning, ladies and gentlemen. Today is an important day for our country. As you all know, we have been dealing with a national health crisis for almost two years now. Although we were able to fast-track a few vaccines to slow the transmission of this terrible disease, its many mutations have continued to plague us.

Fortunately, a brilliant scientist, Chris Cummings, and his staff have developed a unique therapy that, among other important benefits, will protect those who receive it from ever succumbing to the virus. News of this important discovery has received a lot of attention over the past few months, and we have endeavored to negotiate with Dr. Cummings to make the therapy universally available. However, those negotiations have come to a standstill. Consequently, our only recourse is to use the powers granted to me under several national emergency acts to confiscate the research by force. As I speak, the National Guard is entering the Cummings Clinic to retrieve all the salient information and research. We will also be detaining all of its employees to help us facilitate the distribution of this therapy through several large pharmaceutical companies that will be selected by the FDA. All Americans will now have the opportunity to receive this incredible therapy. As you know, this is not an inexpensive treatment. We have already been working with Congress to approve a subsidy program to cover the costs associated with its distribution. Any family whose income is less than $75,000 a year will receive the treatment for free.

Those making more than that will pay only one percent of their income for the treatment. In other words, if your family makes one hundred thousand dollars a year, you will only pay one thousand dollars for the treatment. We expect the FDA to make its selection within a couple of weeks based on bid submissions from various companies. Immediately thereafter they will begin preparations, which we believe will allow a full-scale implementation within six weeks. Now all Americans will have the wonderful benefits associated with this important discovery. Indeed this is a great day for America. Thank you."

He left the podium without taking questions. At the same time, the National Guard was entering the Cummings Clinic and boxing up all the files and materials and equipment. Employees of the HHS were on hand to facilitate their work and meet with the clinic's employees as they began to arrive shortly thereafter. They were informed that they would be required to work directly with the HHS to make sure there was an orderly transfer of the technology to other major companies. They would continue to be paid the same salaries they were currently receiving until the transfer was complete. A that time they would be allowed to pursue other employment opportunities, but of course, the companies providing the treatment were sure to need employees to aid in their efforts to distribute the therapy.

Later the same day the FDA issued a statement offering pharmaceutical companies the opportunity to submit proposals to be selected as companies that would receive the Cummings research. Interested companies were directed to the FDA website where applications were available. The Dartpong companies had developed the applications in a manner that would preclude most competitors and ensure that their submissions would be considered the best.

Everything was going as planned, except Chris and Susan Cummings were nowhere to be found. HHS, the National Guard and almost every news organization were looking for them. It was as if they had disappeared from the earth. Airlines and customs were checked, but there was no sign that they had left the country. Milton even tried to call Chris' personal cell phone. He wanted to apologize for what he had to do, but no answer.

tein called Milton to congratulate him on his efforts to take over the technology, but he was concerned about Chris and Susan's disappearance. "Why have they gone missing and how would they have known ahead of time about our plan?" he asked.

"I have no idea about either," Milton replied.

"Well, somebody had to give them a head's up. Who else knew the details and timing of the raid?"

"Of course, there were a lot of people in on the actual planning, but I can't imagine any of those would have been responsible for the leak."

"Anyone not connected to the preparation have knowledge of it?"

"No one…oh, maybe one person."

"Who?"

"A woman I spend some time with. But she only knew about it the night before the raid and she wouldn't even know how to contact Chris."

"What's her name," he demanded.

"Crystal, Crystal Devore. I'm not even sure that's her real name. She would have no reason to tell him, anyway."

"We can't have loose ends, Milton. Call her and tell her to meet you at the same hotel tomorrow night. I'll take care of the rest."

"Is that really necessary?"

"Yes, it is."

First he had to stab an old friend in the back and now set up his mistress for who knows what. Milton anguished for a few minutes over what he had to do before making the call. He got her voicemail and asked her to call back as soon as possible. He was actually relieved she didn't answer.

A few hours passed and she didn't call back, which was very unusual. He began to wonder if she had gone missing, too. At the same time he was kind of glad she didn't, but soon realized Stein would be upset if she didn't show the next evening. He began to panic and decided to call his father for advice.

"Milton, good to hear your voice. I thought you would be too busy to call dear old Dad. Congrats on the successful raid."

"Thanks Dad, but I have little problem I wanted your advice on."

"Sure son, whatever I can do."

"Albert Stein is upset that it's possible that a woman I spend some time with may have alerted Chris Cummings to our plan, which gave him time to prepare for it. He instructed me to have her be someplace tomorrow night so he could tie up loose ends, but I can't reach her. She always gets back to me within an hour and it's been over four hours already."

"Do you think it's possible that she contacted Chris?"

"I don't think so, but I did tell her about the plan the night before the raid. I just don't know what would motivate her to do it or how she would have known how to reach him."

"What's her name, son?"

"Crystal Devore, at least what she told me her name was."

"Okay, get back to work and I'll take care of it."

"You sure?"

"Yes, just do your job and let me worry about this."

"Thanks, Dad."

CHAPTER 48

Crystal received a text from an unknown number with some specific instructions. She was to pack up all her important things and be in front of Washington's Union Train Station at eight am the following morning. Someone wearing a black overcoat with a felt hat would meet her there. He would recognize her. It was signed Chris Cummings and included a big thank you.

Apparently, Chris thought her warning may put her in danger so she heeded his advice and packed up all her belongings. The next morning she called a cab and dragged two large suitcases to the curb. A black sedan pulled up in front of her apartment building just as she was getting in the cab.

"Where to?" the taxi driver questioned.

"Union Station, please,"

"Sure thing. Not much traffic this morning, should only take fifteen minutes."

As they started towards Massachusetts Avenue, where the Station is located, the black sedan followed close behind. As promised, they arrived at the Station in about fifteen minutes. As Crystal exited the cab she rounded up her suitcases and started towards the station entrance. At the same time a man jumped out of the passenger side of the black sedan and ran towards her. The heavy suitcases slowed her progress and made it easy for the well-dressed man to catch her before she reached the entrance.

"Are you Crystal?" the man asked.

"Yes, did Chris send you?"

"Yes Ma'am, he did. Please follow me, I have a car over here."

"But I thought we were taking a train, and weren't you supposed to be wearing a black overcoat?"

"Yes I was but my wife had my coat in her car. Sorry for the confusion. Last minute change of plans. This will be safer."

"Of course, who else would know I'd be here? I'm sure you guys know what you are doing. I sure appreciate your help."

"Let me help you with your bags," he said as he grabbed both suitcases from Crystal. "That black sedan over there is waiting for us."

With both hands now occupied, it was easier for Chris's real colleague to quickly intervene and incapacitate the potential captor as they headed back to the waiting sedan.

Crystal screamed as the newcomer knocked down her supposed helper. He grabbed both suitcases and yelled, "Follow me. Chris sent me."

Crystal hesitated not knowing for sure which person was really here to help her. But when a bullet whizzed by them, which came from the direction of the waiting black sedan, she figured out quickly who to trust. And, of course, he was wearing a black overcoat with a felt hat. *How stupid*, she thought.

They ran as fast as possible inside the Station and quickly got lost among the other travelers. The potential captor recovered quickly and ran after them, but lost them in the crowd.

CHAPTER 49

Unlike most things in Washington, the subsidy program approval was proceeding quickly. Even the fiscally conservative Republicans had no choice but to jump onboard. There were a few holdouts that objected to the whole process on principal, but in the end the legislation passed by wide margins in both houses, and the president signed the law immediately upon presentation to the White House.

Director Graham and his staff began reviewing the applications even before the legislation was passed. With his prodding, the staff selected ten companies to receive the license to offer the therapy. The agreed price was the average price offered by the ten selected companies. Eight of the ten were Dartpong companies.

Within another month all ten companies had set up clinics to administer The Procedure. The first clinic was set up in Washington, DC by Trident. As a symbolic gesture for his part in making this happen, Secretary Simon was the first to receive the treatment. Other influential politicians followed and to make sure the optics were right, they had dozens of poor citizens in line to receive theirs. One of those was Mrs.

Peter Junkin. Her illness had progressed to the point where she needed to be pushed in a wheelchair into the clinic.

Stacy had flown to Washington to report on the festivities for the *Times*. She knew this would be her last assignment, since she had decided to leave the paper. She noticed the man pushing the wheelchair was wearing a Giants baseball cap. It was indeed Peter Junkin. *It couldn't be a coincidence that his wife was one of the first to receive the therapy.*

The rest of the new clinics were in line to open the following week. But that never happened.

CHAPTER 50

Data continued to pour in from local hospitals. It was now clear that all those inflicted had received The Procedure. Dr. Reed concluded that something had gone wrong with the way The Procedure had been administered, so he asked his staff to run down every original Cummings Clinic employee and get them to participate in a Zoom call. He also told them to keep trying to reach Dr. Cummings.

A few hours later they had been able to round up twelve employees of the Cummings Clinic. Dr. Reed introduced himself to the assembled Zoom participants and explained what was happening. "Do any of you have any idea why this is happening?"

"We have never had any adverse reactions to the therapy when we oversaw it. I can't imagine what could be causing this mass problem," one of the employees offered.

"The only thing I can imagine is that you are not properly administering it," another said.

"But you all were the ones that performed the previous treatments, and from what I understand you trained the new staff."

"That's true, but none of us ever performed the final step in the process."

"Who did?" asked Dr. Reed.

"It was always performed by Chris and Susan."

"But you had their research and specific instructions."

"We didn't have it. They kept the part that they were responsible for locked up in their office in a red binder. The National Guard took it the day they raided our clinic."

"Is it possible that the information in that binder could have been altered and the modification could cause the problems we are seeing now?"

"It's certainly possible. But who would modify it?" asked Dr. Reed.

"Only two people would have had access to it before it was confiscated."

"Then we have to find the Cummingses, or these people will start dying," Reed said as he closed the meeting.

Dr. Reed called the White House and brought them up to speed on what he had found out. Without the Cummingses, they had no ideas on how to help these people. The president's dhief of staff asked the doctor to come to the White House immediately and meet with the president and other high-ranking officials to discuss their options. He agreed.

By the time Dr. Reed arrived at the White House, the oval office was full of people. They had already been briefed. The president started by asking Dr. Reed directly if there was any possible medical solution to the problem.

"There might be, but it will take way too long to figure out. These patients will be dead by then."

"So you're saying the only solution is to find the Cummingses."

"Yes, Mr. President."

The President turned to the rest of the gathered group. "What have we done to try and locate them?"

The National Security Advisor replied, "We have done everything possible. They've just disappeared."

"They must be seeing what is happening. Why wouldn't they want to help? After all, it is their therapy which has caused this."

"I'm not sure they look at it that way, sir," said the Attorney General.

"Why not?" the president questioned.

"Well, we did steal their research and apparently we are not administering their therapy exactly."

"But the changes they made to their treatment book are apparently causing these people to be sick."

"You're correct, but I think they may have a different perspective. I think we need to hold a press conference and appeal to their better instincts. We can offer them immunity if they surrender themselves and provide us the necessary means to help these patients," the Attorney General offered.

"Unfortunately, that seems our only course of action. Get it done right away. You and Dr. Reed should be our spokesmen," said the president.

With the next step in place the group filed out of the oval office and the Attorney General's staff took care of the logistics for the press conference. They decided to hold it in the Rose Garden. Within the hour the press had assembled for the makeshift press briefing. Dr. Reed and the Attorney General spent about fifteen minutes, bringing the press up to date and then appealed to the Cummingses, if they saw this, to come forward. As discussed, they offered them full immunity. If the Cummingses were listening to any news, they would see this since it was broadcast several times over every network.

No one heard anything from the Cummingses for days. Unfortunately, some of the patients began to die, including Peter Junkin's wife. She already was sick, so she succumbed more quickly than others. Patients' families were making appeals to the Cummingses constantly. Lucy Simon begged Chris to come home from wherever he was and save her husband. What nobody but Chris and Susan knew was that the effects were irreversible.

Peter Junkin buried his wife in a family plot outside of Rockville, Maryland. It was where her mother and father were buried. He alone attended the brief ceremony at the local funeral parlor and placed a dozen roses, her favorites, on her grave as the coffin was lowered into its final resting place.

From there he drove home and got out a few pieces of paper and a pen and began to write. When he was finished, he drove to the local UPS store and had the document notarized. Then he placed it in an envelope and addressed it to Stacy Ogden, in care of the *New York Times*. He mailed it from the UPS store, returned to the house, and shot himself.

CHAPTER 51

Chris and Susan did see the news. She finally convinced him to send a reply. He spent a day putting his thoughts together and set up in a non-descript location to video his response. With Susan holding the video camera he provided the following unscripted retort.

"First, let me say that if I came back or not, the patients who received my stolen therapy will not get better. The effects of their treatment are irreversible. But I am compelled to respond to my former country's immunity offer. From what am I offered immunity? What has been my crime? What is the charge against me? Has anyone I sold my procedure to suffered any harm? Has anyone I performed a procedure on had any medical malady? Did I sell my therapy to the government and therefore have an obligation to warrant its effectiveness?

"To the contrary, all the patients who paid me for my procedure have excellent results. The only people who now suffer are those who, through the force of their government, attempted to steal my discovery. They stole the product of my mind. They raided my clinic to confiscate the product of my energy, my time, my effort, and my investment. And they did this with the blessing of most of you.

"But what nobody knew was that I was prepared for that potentiality. I was always concerned that someone would one day attempt to take my property, so I kept the last important step of my procedure completely secret. Not even my closest colleagues were provided this information. Only my wife and I knew how to complete the treatment so that it would provide the desired results. Without this step, as you have now clearly witnessed, the results would actually produce a less favorable outcome.

"So am I now charged with withholding the product of my mind? Do I have a legal obligation to aid those who robbed me? Do I have an ethical responsibility to give away the fruits of my labor? Is it unfair to expect a return on my financial and lifetime investment?

"And, if so, who will be the next person to risk their capital and effort and time to create another breakthrough, if the majority of their elected representatives can at any time confiscate that property merely by suggesting a national emergency?

"Many suggest I am selfish for not sharing my discovery with the world. Many say I put my own self-interest ahead of the community's. But it was my self-interest that created the discovery. If not for self-interest, no one would work and sacrifice to create something of real value. A consequence of all true self-interest is a benefit to all who appropriately pay for it. Great athletes don't work and practice extremely hard in order to play for a minimum salary. Great doctors don't go to school for over 25 years to perform surgery for free. And inventors don't spend countless hours and years of financial sacrifice to create products that are given away or stolen.

"It is self-interest which creates the best athletes, the best products, the best innovations, and ultimately the best standard of living for the greatest number. History clearly shows that the highest standard of living, the greatest innovations, have come from those countries that allow those who pursue their own self-interest to prosper. Self-interest is not the villain, as many have suggested. Self-interest is the driver of progress and innovation.

"I was not given the time to fully recover my financial investment, not to mention my effort, required for this important discovery. But I do not need your immunity. I have enough money to enjoy the rest of my life. And so I close by saying that you will never have the fruits of my mind. Not for this discovery or any new ones. You may have also sent a message to others who are now dissuaded from the sacrifice required to develop other innovations in many areas. You must decide if your future is better off by promoting self-interest or by villainizing it."

CHAPTER 52

Stacy was clearing out her desk as the mail room person dropped off a letter addressed to her. It had no return address. She paused her packing to open the letter. It was handwritten on two pages. She jumped to the end to see who it was from. Peter Junkin must have sent this right before he committed suicide. She had read about his demise just yesterday.

She read the letter intently. It said the following:

Dear Ms. Ogden,

Let me apologize for sending you away last month when you came to my house. At that time I was still hiding my participation in much illegal activity. My wife was extremely sick, and I needed to be around to take care of her. But now that she has passed there is no longer any need to hide my activity.

Let me start by stating that I have been working for Albert Stein of Trident Pharmaceuticals for almost thirty years. I did many bad things that he instructed me to do because I needed the money to help my wife, who had an incurable disease. In the beginning, he promised to provide me enough resources to care for my wife and ultimately promised me that she would be one of the first to receive The Procedure when it became available from his firm.

Before leaving this earth to join my wife, I want to confess to all that I did at the sole direction of Albert Stein and provide you corroboration of other activities of him and his colleagues. First, I or colleagues hired by me, were responsible for all the lab explosions twenty-five years ago. I also was responsible for blowing up the Cummings Lab. All of these acts were done in order to slow the progress of therapies that would reduce the market for drugs provided by Stein's and his colleagues' companies.

Second, at Stein's orders, I tampered with the brakes on Director Graham's assistant's car. I think her name was Grace. I set up detour signs so that she would have to drive on the winding, hilly roads on her way home. I found her by following you. Actually, I had been following you for years. Stein wanted updated reports on what you were discovering and who you were talking to.

Third, I killed Tommy Abbott, the computer hacker who helped you uncover information about Dartpong, LLC. Stein couldn't let you get telephone records that would demonstrate his connection with several other important players. Again, I found him by following you. But you shouldn't feel bad about your role. You were only doing what was right, trying to expose these wicked men.

Fourth, you should know, if you already don't, that Stein is in cahoots with Secretary Simon, Director Graham of the FDA, Martin Grimes at your paper and several other congresspeople who receive significant contributions from their Super PAC – Health for America. He also was providing insider information to Theodore Simon about drug company news soon to be released from the FDA. Simon would use this information to benefit the offshore Dartpong subsidiary and his own hedge fund.

Lastly, Stein, in conjunction with Secretary Simon and his other cohorts, developed the plan to confiscate Cummings research. It was also Stein who rigged the bidding process for The Procedure to ensure he and his colleagues would be selected to deliver the treatments.

I hope this letter will allow you to make all of this public and eventually have the authorities prosecute these crooks. It kills me to know that I spent most of my life working with Stein to try and help my wife and in the end, it ended up killing her. I will never forgive myself for that and the atrocities I committed. May God have mercy on my soul."

It was signed by him and he had had it notarized. She placed the letter in her purse and finished packing up quickly and left. Now she had concrete corroboration and she wasn't about to give it to the *Times*.

When she arrived back at her apartment, she immediately began editing her original article to include this new information. It took her about four hours to finish. Then she had to decide how to get it published. After considering a few alternatives, she called up one of the editors in the New York office of the *Wall Street Journal* and requested a meeting to discuss a groundbreaking story. Based on her reputation, the editor agreed to meet the following morning.

The next morning Stacy packed up all her research, including the notarized letter from Junkin, and took a cab to the *Wall Street Journal* office. At her meeting with the editor, she laid out everything. The last thing she showed him was Peter Junkin's letter. The editor was overwhelmed with her research and the fact that she had been provided concrete corroboration. It was obvious from the letter why she had not submitted this to the *Times*.

While she was there, he called a meeting of the publisher and the paper's chief editor. They all met in their large main conference room, where Stacy went through everything again for the new players.

It was agreed that they would run the piece with Stacy named as a contributing reporter. They agreed to pay her $20,000 for the article, which certainly would come in handy, since she was currently unemployed.

The story ran the following day and all the networks picked it up. Stacy had six major network interview requests immediately. She spent the next three days doing these interviews. While Stacy was becoming a news celebrity, many others were running for cover. None of the people from her article granted an on-air interview and all issued flat denials.

The U.S Justice Department started multiple investigations. The president, in an effort to distance himself, demanded Milton Simon's immediate resignation, which of course, he was in no position to give since he was on his death bed at Walter Reed Medical Center. Director Graham of the FDA resigned of his own accord, seeing the writing on the wall. Theodore Simon was stopped at the airport as he was trying to fly to a non-extradition country.

Albert Stein continued to issue flat denials and hid behind multiple lawyers. A few of his colleagues were considering deals to reduce their potential sentences in return for testimony against their former leader. Unfortunately for them, they had a lot less in financial resources as a result of their last trade.

Right before their companies were selected to administer The Procedure, Theodore Simon had placed huge call option trades for the Dartpong offshore entity and the CEOs' personal accounts. When everything went tits up, the call options became worthless and their accounts became insignificant.

EPILOGUE

Everyone got their just desserts. All the drug companies' executives, including Stein, ended up in jail. Stein got the longest sentence, as it was determined he was the real ringleader. Theodore Milton had to bury his son and was convicted of insider trading. Martin Grimes was fired by the *Times* and couldn't get a job anywhere. Stacy Ogden won her first Pulitzer prize, which made her parents enormously proud. Chris and Susan were doing very well. They took all the cash they had accumulated over the previous eighteen months and bought put options on the eight pharmaceutical companies that were in on the gig. When the companies' stock cratered because of their CEO exposed activity, they made over one hundred million dollars in profits.

Even their investors and employees made out. The papers they had sent to their lawyers on their last night in the clinic was a surrender of their shares in Cummings Lab. As a result, the remaining shareholders owned a much larger percentage of the company. Eventually, the legal procedure following the eminent domain confiscation required the government to pay a reasonable amount for taking the property. All of the remaining shareholders split millions of dollars.

Crystal received her reward, too. She was currently living in a fully paid for two-bedroom flat in Paris and with the monthly distributions from the trust set up by Chris on her behalf, she led a very comfortable life without having to submit to anyone again.

Fifteen Years Later

The United States had become a shadow of its original self. Over the last fifteen years the country had faced two more pandemics. The economy suffered greatly from additional shutdowns mandated by the country's leaders. The additional healthcare costs and stimulus packages drove the national debt to almost one hundred trillion dollars, over four times the nation's gross domestic product. This led to additional consequences: higher interest rates, a reignited inflation, high unemployment, and higher taxes.

It became a malevolent snowball. Higher interest rates increased the mounting national deficits, which increased inflation, which increased social security payments which are adjusted to inflation, which further increased the debt, and led to even higher debt and inflation.

With less money available after debt interest payments, the country's infrastructure grew even worse. Potholes were commonplace in major city streets. Older bridges became unnavigable. National parks were closed.

Even some smaller airports were closed when Federal Aviation Authority budgets were cut.

As federal tax rates approached eighty percent, the wealthy began to ex-patriate, creating even larger deficits. Those that remained lost the incentive to create, innovate, or produce anything of value. But two things remained the same. First, all the elected officials associated with the healthcare scandal of fifteen years ago were still in office. And second, their proposed solutions always involved government action and mandates instead of unleashing the ingenuity of the American people.

Eventually, enough people felt the pain and began to realize that their government could not solve all their problems. Stimulus after stimulus payments did not ease the homeless problem or reduce the growing unemployment. Its massive deficits only caused hyper-inflation, which financially crippled retirees on fixed incomes. A new breed of politician arose from the chaotic landscape. Brave men and women who were willing to stand up to the political establishment which had created the country's decline, began to promote non-government solutions. Their innovative ideas began to catch on and more and more were elected to serve at all levels of government. Hope was on the horizon.

A well-tanned Chris and Susan were watching the news by satellite from their private South Pacific island. They didn't look like they had aged a bit. The CNN reporter was discussing the precarious financial position of the United States.

Healthcare costs as a percentage of GDP had grown to over thirty five percent. One of the show's panelists was admitting that that level of healthcare cost was unsustainable. If it continued at that pace, the economy would be crippled even further. Another panelist offered that if the country had only compensated Chris Cummings fifteen years ago properly for his discovery, we would not be in this mess today. Over the past fifteen years the government's direct and indirect costs of healthcare was almost fifty trillion dollars. We could have paid him a couple of trillion and avoided all of this.

The first panelist said, "Why should we have paid him that much?"

"Because it would have been worth it," was the reply.

As Chris and Susan watched the interview end, she turned with a smile to Chris and asked, "Should we give it to them now?"

Made in the USA
Las Vegas, NV
29 June 2022

50861707R00184